THE
GINGERBREAD
HOUSE

Other Books by Nell Carson

Tell-All

THE GINGERBREAD HOUSE

•

Nell Carson

AVALON BOOKS
NEW YORK

Library of Congress Cataloging-in-Publication Data

Carson, Nell.
    The gingerbread house / Nell Carson.
        p.   cm.
    ISBN 978-0-8034-7469-7 (hardcover : acid-free
paper)   1. Bridal shops—Fiction.   I. Title.
    PS3603.A77625G56 2012
    813'.6—dc23
                                                                2011040004

PRINTED IN THE UNITED STATES OF AMERICA
ON ACID-FREE PAPER
BY RR DONNELLEY, HARRISONBURG, VIRGINIA

To Trish and Gaylene,
thanks for all your support and encouragement!

Prologue

It was time.

Zachary Clemens exhaled a breath in pure satisfaction as he picked up the last piece of wood from the porch railing. He'd spent hours on it yesterday, first carving it down to a smooth finish, then brushing on three coats of glossy black paint—all in preparation for this moment.

Zachary walked over to the front door and swung it open. It still jerked a little at the start. He'd need to work on that. But not today.

Ducking his head inside he called out, "Eliza, it's time!"

No response.

But was that titters of laughter trickling down from upstairs?

"Lizzie?"

"We'll be just a minute, dear," his wife's voice sang out. "Go on now and wait outside."

She was up to something. Zachary heard it in her voice. Smiling, he breathed in the fresh pine scent that wafted through the entire house, and then he headed back outside to the porch.

Leaning against the post by the stairs, he fingered the

piece of wood, just itching to put it in its place. From inside, he at last heard the sound of footsteps coming down the stairs.

The front door opened and there she was, his beautiful wife, Eliza, together with their five-year-old daughter, Jane, and three-year-old son, William. Six-month-old Isabelle was nestled in Lizzie's arms, sleeping peacefully as she had all summer, despite the hammering and sawing that had filled the air nearly every day.

Zachary's mouth dropped open in surprise. Every last one of them was dressed in their Sunday best, complete with clean shiny hair and freshly scrubbed faces. Isabelle's hair, usually a frizzy mop of blond curls, was smoothed down around her precious little ears.

"But today's Tuesday!"

Beaming, Lizzie nodded. "Yes, but it's certainly an occasion!" She kissed him on the cheek while Will and Janie latched on to both of his legs.

Zachary grinned. "All right, then, let's finish this."

Pulling a penny nail from the pocket of his carpenter's apron, he lumbered over to the top of the porch steps, his older children still attached to his legs.

As his family watched with eager eyes, Zachary reached up and carefully positioned the gleaming black number 2 to the right of the 3. He set the nail against it.

"Will? My hammer please."

His eyes wide at the important task bestowed upon him, Will reached up to the loop of his father's tool belt, pulled out the hammer, and handed it up to him.

Stifling a grin at the solemn expression on his son's face,

Zachary took the hammer and tapped lightly on the nail in the center of the number to anchor it. "Ready?" Everyone nodded.

As Zachary drove the nail home, Lizzie and the children shouted, "Hurrah!"

"Now, come," Lizzie said, taking hold of his hand. "Let's take a look at this new house of ours."

Zachary allowed her to tug him down the stairs, still encumbered by Will and Janie. They screamed with laughter as their father lurched them down the new brick path he'd finished laying just the week before. He stopped halfway and turned around. Will and Jane finally let go and stood up.

Zachary slipped his arm around Lizzie's waist but quickly withdrew it. He was still grimy and sweaty from working all day, finishing up the seemingly endless row of gingerbread along the front eave. "Sorry, dear. I hope I haven't mussed your dress."

"Oh, Zachary, never mind that now," Lizzie scolded. She took his hand and wrapped it firmly back around her waist.

For a moment the four of them gazed up at the house. "It's wonderful," Lizzie whispered. "Just wonderful."

And it was, the dream house they'd always talked about, three stories complete with a dramatic steepled turret, a wraparound porch and, of course, the gingerbread decorating all the eaves.

Zachary had built the house with his own two hands along with the help of his two brothers, both carpenters by trade before their claim came in. He could have hired someone else to build it, but he'd wanted to do it himself. And he was glad he had.

He nodded. "It'll do."

Lizzie laughed delightedly at his understatement and squeezed his hand. "It most certainly will."

Chapter One

It was time.

The bell in the clock tower overhead tolled three times, solemn and slow, like a death knell. Appropriate enough.

As Mayor Anita Cox lifted her gavel, Greta Kendall swallowed hard once again, trying to quash the thickening lump in her throat. For days she'd known this was coming, yet that had done nothing to help her prepare for this moment.

Beside her on the long bench, her lawyer, Jack Fenton, young and impossibly handsome, lay his hand comfortingly over hers.

Mayor Cox had to bang her gavel down several times to quiet the room. Never before had so many people squeezed inside the town council chambers, every last seat taken with a couple dozen folks standing by the back wall and along the side aisles. On the way here, Greta had seen quite a few CLOSED signs on shop doors along Main Street. She wasn't surprised. It was quite a moment for Spector, Colorado. Pivotal really.

For the past hour everyone had sat fidgeting through a seemingly endless agenda—a new noise ordinance, a parking rate increase, an extension of a utility easement. Greta heard yawns from all around her.

Mayor Cox cleared her throat and took on that officious manner Greta remembered well from high school. Anita had been class president all four years, running unopposed the last two.

"And now, the last item on the council agenda: a final vote on Resolution 32A regarding approval of the proposed site plan as submitted by Harwood Development." Gosh, it sounded so innocuous when put like that.

Greta sat up straighter and let out a long, slow breath, trying to calm her heart hammering away in her chest.

Mayor Cox nodded at the woman at the far end of the platform on which the seven council members were seated with Cox in the center. "Councillor Simmons, what is your vote?"

"Yea."

"Councillor Chen?"

"Yea."

Cox proceeded down the line of the council members, each "yea" like a dagger to Greta's chest. Still, she wasn't surprised. She'd known, heck, the entire town had known, how the council would vote, every last one of them eager for the fresh revenue they anticipated flowing into Spector.

Greta flinched as Cox banged her blasted gavel once again. "The motion has been passed unanimously."

Beside her, Jack stood up and raised his hand. Cox nodded down to him. "Exceptions are duly noted in the record."

Cox seemed to be making a point of avoiding eye contact with Greta. Even as fresh tears burned her eyes, Greta tried to catch the mayor's eye, wanted her to *see*, to acknowledge what she and the other council members had just done to her life.

But Cox looked beyond her to the rest of the room. "There being no further business before this council at this time, by motion regularly adopted, the town council of Spector, Colorado, stands adjourned."

She banged her gavel one last time, gathered her things, and stepped off the platform, disappearing through a side door. Coward.

"Finally. Thank God *that's* over with."

Greta knew that voice, her ears zeroing in on it even through the excited murmurs of the crowd. She closed her eyes and tilted her head to the other side, not wanting to catch even a glimpse of that horrible woman.

"Oh, Greta, honey, I'm so sorry."

Greta opened her eyes to see Penny Grindbold, her best friend since kindergarten, standing in front of her, eight months pregnant with her first child. Penny's green eyes, usually sparkling with excitement during the past few months, were now awash in sympathy. Greta jerked her gaze away from her. She couldn't see that pity in Penny's face, didn't want to cry here. Especially in front of that woman. She wouldn't give her the satisfaction.

"Thanks, Pen," Greta mumbled, still averting her eyes from Penny.

She stood up and felt her knees falter beneath her. Jack grabbed her arm. "Greta? Are you all right?"

"Just get me out of here, please?" Her voice was weak, her strength completely depleted.

"Absolutely," Jack said, putting an arm around her waist.

Supported by Penny on one side and Jack on the other,

Greta made her way through the crowd keeping her head down, not wanting to meet anyone's eyes, unable to bear the pity she knew she'd find there as well.

When she saw the manila envelope in her mailbox with no return address, she almost didn't open it. Greta figured it was from him and was about to rip it up.

But then she noticed there was also no postage and no postmark on it. It had been hand delivered, her name and address neatly typed on the label. No way could he have gotten someone to come all the way up to Spector.

Still, Greta hesitated before slipping her thumb under the flap. He could be mighty persuasive when he wanted to be. She hated feeling controlled like this, manipulated, even from so far away.

Jaw set, she ripped open the envelope and held her breath as she unfolded the piece of paper she found inside.

It was a copy of a birth certificate. Very old, from 1896. She read the name at the top. Leonard Bartland-Russell. The writer?

Quickly, Greta scanned the certificate. Her mouth dropped open when she saw the address: 132 Lamont Street. Her house!

She peered into the envelope again, saw a piece of notepaper inside and slid it out. Unfamiliar handwriting, slanted far to the right, and very precise.

Good luck. A friend.

Greta's face split into a huge smile. "Yes!" She burst inside the house. "Mom! Guess what?"

Chapter Two

A bull in a china shop? A fish out of water? No, Greta mused, more like a hippie at a gun show.

However you wanted to say it, she knew one thing for sure: *That man is out of his comfort zone.*

Greta put out her CLOSED FROM 1:30 TO 3:30 sign and watched as he browsed through the bridal dresses and veils, trying very hard to look like it was the most natural thing in the world for him to be doing. A smile perked up the edges of Greta's mouth. He probably wouldn't know the difference between charmeuse and chiffon.

He was good-looking, though, her newest customer. Around thirty like herself, dark eyes—brown or maybe a deep blue—set in a face that had that permanent-looking tan common to devout skiers, as most people were around here, with Aspen only ten miles "down the hill," as the people of Spector liked to say.

And he looked Aspen-y, didn't he, with his Oakleys hanging on a green and blue cord around his neck, khaki pants, and a black fleece sweatshirt. Slung unexpectedly across one arm was a white dress bag.

Finished with his appraisal of her selection of wedding gowns, he meandered over to the other side of the store—and right into the lingerie section.

Finding himself suddenly surrounded by a vast assortment of delicate bras and panties, garters and slips, the man coughed lightly, bright red splotching across his chiseled cheekbones.

Squelching her smile, Greta walked around the counter and headed over to him as he made a show of repositioning the dress bag exactly three inches across his arm.

"Can I help you?" Greta tried to instill a professional tone in her voice in an effort to alleviate some of his embarrassment. He jumped a little and she took a step back. "Sorry, I didn't mean to startle you."

"No, you're fine." The words sounded as if they'd been squeezed through a tight throat. "I'm waiting for someone."

"Ah. All right then, how about some coffee while you wait? Or tea?"

"No, thanks." The dress bag brushed against a pink satin bra, and it began teetering back and forth precariously on the rack. The man jerked sideways in a valiant effort to save the bra, but he almost dropped the dress bag in the process. Greta leaned over and steadied the bra with one finger and then smiled at the man.

"How about a Scotch?"

Surprised, he finally made full eye contact with her.

Blue. His eyes were midnight blue, almost black.

And familiar? Greta studied his face for a moment but couldn't quite place him.

As the man realized she was joking, a smile eased the tight line of his lips. He held out his free hand to her. "I'm Gray Daniels." The name also struck her as familiar, but in a vague kind of way.

"Nice to meet you, Gray. I'm Greta Kendall." Greta smiled, feeling the dampness of his palm against hers. But then she caught sight of the faded Art Deco–style letters printed across the dress bag and her eyes widened. "Is that a Mainbocher? A *vintage* Mainbocher?"

Pride swept through Gray's eyes. "It sure is. A 1947 original."

Greta couldn't take her eyes off the bag. "But he only designed for movie stars and royalty back then."

Gray nodded. "My grandmother was Eleanor Broussard's personal assistant. Ms. Broussard commissioned Mainbocher to make her wedding dress the year she won her first Academy Award. But then her fiancé met someone else at a post-Oscars party and unceremoniously dumped her. The next morning she said to my grandmother, 'Take it—you can have it. Just get it out of my sight.' It just so happened my grandmother was marrying my grandfather that spring and needed a dress."

"Oh, wow." Greta suddenly felt giddy, like a little girl on Christmas morning. "Can I see it?"

"It needs a little work. That's why I brought it. I hear you're something of a bead expert."

Greta shook her head. "That's my mother." She had tried to learn the craft herself as a little girl, but she hadn't inherited the easy sureness of her mother's hands, her own fingers too clumsy to hold on to the tiny glass spheres.

As Greta rolled a dress form out from the back, Gray unzipped the bag. Together they brought the dress out and carefully tugged it down onto the form. He was right. The dress definitely needed some work.

Oh, but what a dress. It practically took Greta's breath

away. Buttery ivory satin, a bateau neckline, then a smooth skimming drape ending in a brush train. The simplicity of the cut allowed the beadwork covering the bodice to shine.

"It's—it's beautiful," she finally breathed out.

"Isn't it?" Gray said. "My mother wore it as well, when she married my dad. She died last year, but before she did, I promised her Stephanie would wear it."

Greta's shoulders stiffened reflexively. Stephanie. A name she didn't exactly relish at the moment.

"I want her to wear it too," Gray was saying. "It would feel like my mother was there in some way. I really miss her."

Greta heard the catch in his voice and finally tore her gaze away from the dress to look at him. Were those tears gleaming in his eyes? He coughed lightly, clearly embarrassed, a light blush again skimming across his cheekbones. Gosh, he was charming. Gorgeous *and* charming.

And engaged.

Well, she could look, couldn't she? It wasn't like anything was going to happen. They were standing here discussing his fiancée's wedding dress, after all. Besides, she wasn't looking for anything. At all. She'd played that little game and lost.

"Oh, Greta, you *did* bring him!"

Greta cringed. Oh, no. Not again. Her mother came rushing out from her workroom and scurried up to Gray.

"Mom, no." Greta tried to intervene, but it was too late.

"I'm Adele, Adele Kelly," her mother said, pumping Gray's hand up and down. "I'm so glad to finally meet you!" She turned her beaming smile to Greta. "Your father will be so happy."

Greta let out a breath and touched her mother's arm. "Mom, Dad died, remember?" She tried to keep her tone gentle and calm, but it was difficult. She would never get used to these sudden unpredictable jumps in time that her mother's deteriorating mind increasingly took.

"Oh, nonsense," her mother said with a dismissive wave. "He's right upstairs, taking a nap. He was so afraid you two were going to elope. But now you're here. You're here! And so handsome. My, my, those eyes . . ."

"Mom, please," Greta said, cringing again. She wrapped her hand gently around her mother's forearm to lead her back to her workroom, but her mother was having no part of it. She was thin and frail but still had some strength left, and she pulled away easily.

"I'm sorry, Greta, but I'd like to get to know my future son-in-law if you don't mind."

Giving up on her mother, Greta turned to Gray. "I'm so sorry—"

But Gray suddenly bent down and wrapped his arms around her mother in a warm hug. "It's wonderful to finally meet you, Adele. Greta has told me so much about you."

Surprised, Greta only stood there, looking at the two of them.

But as Gray stepped back, he caught her eye and winked. He knew exactly what was going on and was playing along with her mother's fantasy. Well, what could it hurt? In a few moments, any moment really, it could go away. And in this moment, this very moment, her mother was happy. And there had been so much to be unhappy about lately.

Her mother planted her hands on her hips and scowled at them in mock disapproval.

"But you're so far apart. Come, come. Closer, closer." Smiling, she took Greta's hand and Gray's and pulled them together so that they were only a breath away from each other. Gray swung an arm up and around Greta's shoulders, pulling her closer to him, so close she could smell his shampoo. Something citrus, fresh and clean.

"That's better," Adele decided. "Now you look like a real couple. Oh! How about a kiss?"

Greta felt Gray stiffen beside her as a blush grew hot across her entire face. Gray coughed lightly, pulled his arm away and gestured to the dress on the form. "Did you see the dress, Adele?"

Nice deflection. To Greta's relief, Adele shifted her rapturous gaze from the two of them to the dress on the form.

"It was my grandmother's."

"Oh, my, it's a Mainbocher, isn't it? Stunning, absolutely stunning. Greta will look perfect in it! However did you get your hands on it?"

As Gray told her mother about Eleanor Broussard, Greta couldn't help but notice the absolute perfection of his lips, full and smooth-looking and so quick to smile. His complete attention was fixed on Adele, so she felt safe indulging in those lips for just a moment. And then came the thought, utterly of its own accord. *What would it be like to kiss them?*

Greta blinked and looked away from Gray, forcing her gaze back onto the dress. *Down girl*, she chided herself. It had just been such a long time since she'd even been attracted to a man, it had kind of blindsided her.

"My, my," her mother said, making a clucking noise with her tongue, "it does need some work, doesn't it? Quite a bit actually." She pulled away a loose section of cloth from the right side, revealing a gaping hole beneath it.

"Squirrels got to it in our attic in Aspen," Gray explained.

"What a shame," Adele said, but then she brightened. "Don't you worry, though. I'm sure we can get it up to snuff in no time. No time at all. Oh, but I'm being rude. Would you like some tea?" Without waiting for an answer, she started for the kitchen in the back of the house. "Yes, that will be lovely. I'll make us all some tea, and we can have a nice long visit."

And then she was gone, her small frame disappearing into the kitchen.

"Alzheimer's?" Gray asked in a low voice.

Greta nodded. "Early onset. Diagnosed last June."

"My father too. He's a little worse off than your mother. I had to check him into a home this week. Hardest thing I've ever had to do."

"I'm sorry," Greta said and touched his arm. Still, it seemed inadequate. She glanced into his eyes and again saw the glimmer of tears.

Gray visibly swallowed and then lifted his sleeve to check his watch.

Greta drew in a quick breath of air. "Oh, gosh, what time is it?"

"One twenty," Gray answered, his jaw tightening. "She was supposed to be here at one. I'm sorry she's so late. She's getting her 'lowlights retouched,' whatever that means."

Greta bit her lip. The special session was at two o'clock. Sure, it was only a few blocks away, at Spector's town hall, but she could *not* be late. Not today. "I'm sorry, but we may have to reschedule if she's not here soon. I have to be somewhere at two."

Gray nodded. "Me too."

"Actually, though," Greta began with a more critical eye trained on the dress, "I'm not sure we're even ready for a fitting. I'd like to get this hole repaired first. We wouldn't want it getting any worse." She fingered the sides of the hole and looked more closely around the edges of it. "Uh-oh, looks like those squirrels of yours made off with a few strands of beads too. We're going to have to match them, and they may be hard to find. It could get pretty expensive."

Gray shrugged. "I've been specifically told we're sparing no expense when it comes to the wedding." He laughed a bit sheepishly. "That's Stephanie's little joke. 'You're going to be a Harwood now. You need to act the part.' Lately she's taken to calling me 'Mr. Harwood.' Sometimes I think—"

But Greta was no longer listening. "Your fiancée is Stephanie Harwood? Stephanie Bryce Harwood?"

And that was when she heard car doors slamming outside. Three of them, right in a row.

Chapter Three

Frowning, Greta walked up to the door of the shop and looked outside.

There she was. Stephanie Bryce Harwood, Greta's nemesis for the past year, sailing up the walk in all her glory.

A slender, willowy blond, Stephanie was dressed impeccably in a peach-colored suit, from one of Aspen's more exclusive boutiques, no doubt. Her makeup looked professionally done, her lips the latest color from Chanel or Lancôme, as opposed to Greta's usual ChapStick. And unlike her own unruly brown curls, Stephanie's hair was smooth and sleek, framing her stunning, heart-shaped face. All in all, Stephanie always reminded Greta of one of those perfectly coiffed news anchors from the local station—complete with perma-smile.

As the woman approached the front steps, Greta caught a flash of red on the underside of one heel. Louboutins. *Of course.* Greta found herself meanly hoping one of the woman's fancy shoes got caught between bricks and tripped her up. The woman deserved a skinned knee, at the very least.

The Koslovsky brothers, Ian and Gregor, the editors-in-chief of Spector's two feuding newspapers, came bustling up behind her, cameras in hand, excitement shining on their identical faces, Ian's a bit plumper than Gregor's.

Gray muttered, "What the . . . ?" She hadn't realized he'd come up alongside her.

Gray Daniels was Stephanie Harwood's fiancé. No wonder he had looked familiar. She must have seen a photo of him with Stephanie at some point, read his name in the caption.

He swung open the door and strode out onto the porch just as Stephanie reached the top step.

Greta also walked outside, holding the sides of her arms against the chill. What was going on?

"Well, hello, darling!" Stephanie murmured and drew Gray toward her, kissing him lightly on the mouth. In that moment, Greta was horrified to feel a flash of irrational jealousy sear through her. She set her jaw and steeled herself for whatever was going to come next.

Gray leaned down to whisper something in Stephanie's ear.

"Well, I'll tell you what I'm doing, darling," Stephanie began, turning her thousand-kilowatt smile toward the Koslovsky brothers at the bottom of the stairs. They were eagerly snapping pictures, jostling each other for the best angle. As they realized she was about to speak, they let their cameras fall back on their straps and grabbed for their notebooks and pencils. "I'm having my wedding dress made here at this charming little shop, Chantilly Dreams." Greta's scowl deepened as Stephanie's voice took on an infomercial phony brightness.

"I've been told Ms. Kendall's wonderful little shop

here is *the* best bridal store in the area, specializing in hand beading. I'd like everyone to know she'll have a prime spot, right near the entrance. And I'm personally going to tell all my friends to head straight for Chantilly Dreams, whatever their bridal needs."

Then she flashed that special smile of hers, the one Greta had seen dozens of times in both the Koslovskys' papers during her relentless campaign to destroy the great town of Spector.

Once again Ian and Gregor whipped up their cameras and began snapping away as Stephanie posed, one arm possessively around Gray's waist, the other gesturing at the sunflower yellow sign above the porch reading CHANTILLY DREAMS, the words carefully carved into the wood by Greta's grandfather decades earlier.

Greta's grandmother, Bessie, had opened Chantilly Dreams in 1962. At the time, hers was one of only a handful of bridal shops in all of Pitkin County, and so she'd enjoyed a thriving trade. Adele had taken over in the early eighties after Bessie's arthritis had gotten the upper hand, and now it was Greta's joyful responsibility.

"Oh, but now I'm afraid we're going to have to postpone our little fitting," Stephanie said, affecting a forlorn expression. "We don't want to be late, do we?" She nodded at the Koslovskys. "Coming, boys?"

Their balding heads bobbing up and down, Ian and Gregor raced toward their cars. Gregor beat Ian to his car and flashed his twin a triumphant grin.

Shaking her head in disbelief at what had just happened, Greta watched Stephanie stroll toward her white

Escalade, her Louboutins clacking merrily away on the bricks. In front of Greta, Gray stood stock still, watching his fiancée. His back was toward her, so she couldn't see his expression. Greta bet he was smiling from ear to ear in smug satisfaction at pulling off their impromptu press conference.

"Grayson?" Stephanie called, as she swung open the door of the SUV. "Come, darling, don't be late now." Her light blue eyes slid past his shoulder to Greta. Again with that fake smile. "See you there, Ms. Kendall!"

With a little wave, she climbed up into her enormous car and swung the door closed.

Gray turned around to face Greta. His eyes were darker now, more black than blue. She saw no trace of the smile she'd expected. "I'm sorry," he began, "I didn't—"

A sustained honk from the Escalade obscured whatever he said next. He let out a breath and hurried toward his truck, a forest green Ford with an extended cab.

Watching them drive away, Greta knew she should follow, and quickly. But right now she was too furious to do anything but stand there seething on the porch, every muscle in her body tense. She took in a few breaths, trying to calm down. The last few minutes ran over and over in her mind. She'd just *stood* there, allowing that woman to manipulate the situation. Argh! She couldn't stand her.

Greta walked down the stairs and then turned to look up at the house, willing it to give her strength.

God, how she loved the place.

Built in 1889 by a struck-it-rich silver miner, it was a spectacular three-story Queen Anne. Intricately carved

gingerbread, lovingly restored by her grandfather, deco-
rated the undersides of the eaves and the porch.

Her grandparents had moved into the house when Adele
was seven, after their first house at the edge of town was
struck by lightning and burned to the ground. They'd all
gotten out in time and could only stand watching help-
lessly as the flames licked up the sides of the house and
then consumed it. They'd lost everything.

Her grandfather had painted the gingerbread a creamy
ivory and the rest of the house a rich cinnamon brown,
giving the house the appearance of real gingerbread. He'd
wanted Adele to get excited about moving into it and
hoped it would help ease the painful loss of their home. It
had worked. Adele had been thrilled to live in what the
town quickly dubbed the "Gingerbread House." He'd meant
for it to be temporary, but young Adele wouldn't hear of it
being repainted. And so it had remained.

It was so much more than just a house or a place of
business to Greta. It was *home*, as it always had been.
And would continue to be, God willing.

As long as nothing went wrong today. A troublesome
worry had begun worming its way into Greta's belly.
Something in Stephanie's parting smile had bothered her,
something that hinted at triumph.

Greta's hands formed into fists. No, not today, missy.
Today was *her*—Greta's—day. She'd won. Now it just
needed to be made official.

From inside the house, Greta made out the whistling
of the teapot. She'd forgotten all about her mother in the
fierce little storm that was Stephanie Harwood.

She walked quickly up the steps and into the house. "Mom?" she called out as she strode toward the kitchen. "I'm sorry I—"

She stopped as she saw her mother standing by the table, looking down in confusion at the tray she'd prepared.

"Greta, honey? Why are there three cups? Do we have company?"

Chapter Four

Gray finally found a parking spot two and a half blocks from Spector's town hall. He slammed the truck door closed and headed toward the square, his feet pounding on the sidewalk, anger building with each step.

He spotted her in front of the Edwardian-style town hall, holding what looked like his brown jacket. Townspeople streamed all around her into the building.

"*That* was the place?" he demanded when she was within earshot.

"Of course that was the place." Stephanie's carefree shrug only further infuriated him.

"Tell me you didn't do it for the publicity, Stephanie. Tell me you did it because your mother, your aunt, one of your *hordes* of friends told you Chantilly Dreams was the best bridal shop in the area."

She batted her cool blue eyes at him. "Grayson, darling, don't be so dramatic. It was necessary."

"A cheap publicity stunt?"

She arched a brow at him. "An opportunity."

"But this is our wedding!" Several people glanced over at him and he lowered his voice, although rage still sliced through the words. "You'd use our wedding, my grandmother's dress to, to—" He whipped a hand through his hair in hopeless frustration.

With a small smile, Stephanie reached up to pat his hair back down. "Oh, come on, darling. I needed some good press because of the beating she's about to take in there. Half this town's on her side, and we can't have them be all upset and not come to our wonderful mall, now, can we? Now here, I brought your jacket." She pulled down the zipper of his fleece and began tugging it down around his shoulders.

Confused, Gray looked around at the other towns-people heading into the session, most of them in jeans and casual sweaters. And then it dawned on him, and he felt his jaw grow rigid. "Why, Stephanie? Why exactly do I need a jacket?"

"Because, darling, I need you in there." Stephanie had finally succeeded in pulling off his fleece, leaving him in only the white dress shirt she'd laid out for him that morning. She held the jacket up.

Gray let out a breath but took the jacket, mostly because a cool mountain breeze was blowing right through the thin cotton of his shirt. He shrugged on the jacket and watched in disbelief as Stephanie reached into her briefcase and pulled out a blue tie.

"Here, put this on," she said, holding out the tie.

"Stephanie—"

Evidently she heard the warning tone in his voice. She flashed him that saucy smile of hers, the one that reminded him of the mischievous little girl she'd been so many years ago. "What? You're still a lawyer, last time I checked."

"Not for much longer."

"Oh, come on. It'll be easy breezy. In and out. Please? I'll owe you." She rose up on her toes and gave him a quick peck on the lips. Her smile faltered as she felt his lips grow rigid beneath hers. "Please, honey," she began in a more serious voice. "I need your help here. I didn't want to pay one of our lawyers five hundred an hour to do this one simple thing. I have to show my father how cost effective I can be."

"Technically, you don't even need a lawyer for this."

Her crimson lips tightened as impatience flitted through her eyes. "You know I can't do it myself."

Gray chuckled bitterly. "So you want me to do your dirty work."

"Come on, Grayson. It'll be a big favor." She turned the smile up a notch. "Kind of like the favor I did for you when I agreed to let you design Winter's Haven fresh out of architecture school. Remember?"

Gray narrowed his eyes. "And here I thought you'd done that as a show of support. Silly me."

That hit the mark. The forced smile disappeared, her eyes at last showing true emotion. "Please, Gray, I really need this to work out. You know how much it means to me, what's at stake."

He did. Her father, Adam Harwood, was planning to retire in a couple of years, and Stephanie wanted very much to prove to him that she was just as capable of running the family business as her brother, Timothy, head of the Denver branch of Harwood Development.

Timothy was two years younger than Stephanie, yet Adam was clearly grooming him to take over the helm of the company. And Stephanie couldn't exactly throw her hat in the ring when her father didn't even acknowledge she had one to throw.

Adam had always treated her as Daddy's little girl, and that had never changed. She'd tried hard to prove she'd out-grown that stagnant image he had of her, first by graduating magna cum laude from the University of Denver, and then going on to receive her MBA from the Daniels College of Business at D.U., also with honors. She'd been working in the Aspen branch of Harwood Development ever since, but Adam was still very much in charge there. He allowed Stephanie to handle only simple, boilerplate projects.

Trying to impress him, she'd vigorously researched pos-sible projects in and around Pitkin County and had finally come up with the idea for Winter's Haven. After she'd presented the schematics to her father, he'd agreed to fund the project.

Still, Stephanie told Gray it felt like Adam had merely patted her on the head and sent her on her way to failure. And Gray suspected she was right in that. Adam had prob-ably already written off the money, happy to indulge his little girl's latest *kick*.

So now here she was, acting the part of hard-nosed developer, knowing how ruthless her brother was in Den-ver, tearing down old houses, entire neighborhoods even, without a second thought.

Tasting defeat, Gray let out a rush of air. "Fine." His jaw still tight, he grabbed the tie out of her hand, swung it around his neck, and began jerking it together in some semblance of a knot. "She's going to be humiliated, you know. We could have at least warned her."

"Oh, right," Stephanie scoffed, and Gray sighed as the hard-nosed act clicked firmly back into place. "Give away our trump card, hand that cute lawyer of hers a golden opportunity to weasel out of it. Absolutely not. They'll be caught off guard, and it'll be a done deal before you can say 'Grand Opening November First.' We need to break ground, Gray, and soon, in order to open for Christmas next year. Time to put all this behind us, say good-bye to the Gingerbread House. Ridiculous name anyway. What, are we—five years old?" She looked down at her watch. "Come on, we'd better get in there."

She gave him an appraising look, reached up, and fussed with the knot in his tie. A quick nod and she was heading toward the entrance of the building with that fierce determination Gray had once found so endearing. But now people were getting hurt.

Gray looked at his own watch. 1:55. He glanced around the square. Greta would be late if she didn't get here soon. But his shoulders tensed as he realized it didn't matter anyway. She'd already lost.

And then he saw Greta down the block and he let out a breath he didn't realize he'd been holding. Her rich brown curls blew around her face in the breeze, the long ringlets skimming her shoulders as she hurried down the street. She'd added a white linen jacket over the flowing lavender print dress she was wearing in the shop, and it wasn't nearly warm enough for the chilly mountain air of early spring. He suspected she had grabbed the first thing she'd found in her closet, afraid of being late.

The sun ducked behind a cloud, and the temperature

instantly dropped several degrees. As Greta wrapped the jacket tighter around her, Gray frowned miserably. She looked cold and so very vulnerable, especially when he knew what was about to happen.

And he'd be the one to deliver the final blow.

Chapter Five

At exactly one minute before two, Greta swung open the heavy wooden door of the council chambers and rushed inside the room, finding it once again filled to capacity. She knew she was cutting it close, but she'd had to make sure her mother was comfortably settled in her workroom before leaving.

The entire way here, she had tried to block out that last glimpse of her mother's face, the sad, lost look in her eyes. Even more terrible was Adele's awareness of what was happening to her and that it would only get worse. Greta knew that knowledge haunted even her most lucid moments.

As she made her way down the middle aisle, Greta saw Jack seated at the table on the left side. A look of relief passed over his handsome face as he spotted her.

At the table across the aisle sat Stephanie Harwood, and next to her was Gray Daniels, wearing a brown jacket now. He was looking down at some papers on the desk in front of him.

Greta glared at him, but he didn't look over at her. She did notice that he did seem aware of her, though—his shoulders raised, tense, his jaw set.

For this session, instead of the town council members,

the five members of Spector's Landmark Board sat on the raised platform in the front of the room.

The bell in the clock tower overhead rang out two times, and the chairman, Patrick Shaw, began banging his gavel trying to quiet the excited murmurs of the crowd. As usual, it took a few minutes with so many people packed into the room.

For the last two years, Winter's Haven had divided the town, with half bitterly opposed to the mall and half excited about the prospect. Stephanie Harwood's argument had resonated with the latter. She believed the downturn in the economy had been so bad that even Aspen was affected. She argued that people there would love an opportunity to shop somewhere other than the high-end shops populating that town, as long as it was somewhere close by.

The crowd behind them finally quieted, although a buzz of expectant energy still resonated throughout the room.

"The sole item on today's agenda," Patrick Shaw began, speaking slowly and clearly into the microphone, "is the granting of landmark status to the property located at 132 Lamont Street owned by Ms. Greta Kendall, commonly known as the Gingerbread House. Isn't that right, Ms. Kendall?"

Greta nodded. "Yes, Chairman Shaw." It was so odd to call him that. She'd known Patrick since kindergarten. He gave Greta a warm smile, and she saw that the other board members were also smiling down at her. They had to be pleased. She knew every one of them was against the new mall. Patrick had even written an op-ed piece for

Ian's paper in which he talked about Stephanie bulldozing over Spector's history.

"The board has reviewed the materials submitted by Ms. Kendall and Mr. Fenton and is satisfied the applicants have shown the property to indeed be the birthplace of two-time Pulitzer Prize–winning author Leonard Bartland-Russell in January of 1898. The board is further satisfied that the property therefore meets the criteria for historical landmark status under the Historic Preservation Ordinance outlined in the Town of Spector's Revised Code, Section 8-10. The Board hereby—"

"Excuse me, Chairman Shaw, but I'm here to dispute that status." It was Gray Daniels, his chair squeaking against the floor as he stood up. The worry that had taken hold in Greta's stomach began squirming around in there uncomfortably.

Patrick frowned. "And you are . . . ?"

"Grayson Daniels, attorney at law, here on behalf of Harwood Development."

"Uh-oh," Jack muttered beside her.

"What's 'uh-oh'?" Greta whispered worriedly.

"They have something." The certainty in Jack's voice sent a waterfall of dread down Greta's spine.

"And you have something to add to this case?" Patrick was asking Daniels.

"I do."

Jack stood up, his thick brows furrowed in indignation. "Mr. Chairman, this is highly—"

"Yes, yes, I agree," Patrick said, nodding at Jack. He turned toward Gray again. "You understand this is coming extremely late in the process."

"I do, Mr. Chairman, and I apologize for the timing, but the results of a study we commissioned came in only late yesterday."

Patrick covered the microphone with his hand as he conferred with the other members of the board. Greta realized she was holding her breath, and she let it out slowly.

Patrick once again leaned into the microphone. "You may proceed, Mr. Daniels." He sat back and waited expectantly along with the other board members.

All eyes were on Gray Daniels now as he held a photograph up high enough for everyone to see. "This is a photograph of Bartland-Russell's original birth certificate as examined by leading national archivist Desmond Welder. A state-of-the-art technical examination of the certificate has revealed the address of 132 Lamont Street to be incorrect."

As the spectators behind her broke out in excited whispers and gasps, Greta sat back in her chair, stunned. "No, no, no, no, no," she muttered softly. Beside her, Jack took her hand and squeezed it.

"As this photograph makes clear, you will see that the 1 here is actually a 7, the second line previously obscured by a crease in the paper. We believe this newfound evidence unequivocally proves the actual birthplace of Leonard Bartland-Russell to be six blocks to the north, at 732 Lamont Street."

Half the room erupted in cheers, the other half letting out disgruntled mutterings.

"Yes!" That was Gregor Koslovsky, seated in the first row behind her. He punched the air in triumph while beside him, his brother Ian frowned and shook his head.

Winter's Haven Mall had divided not only the town but the two previously inseparable twin brothers. They'd fought bitterly over it and had ended up splitting up the newspaper their great-grandfather had founded into two separate and warring newspapers. The town wasn't really big enough for both of them, but neither would give in.

Greta watched in disbelief as Gray walked up to the platform to hand a copy of the photo to each member of the Landmark Board. He then came over to her table and handed one to Jack, who immediately angled it into the overhead lights to examine it more closely.

Gray then held a copy out for her and automatically Greta took it, her eyes riveted on the black-and-white photograph.

"I'm sorry." Or so she thought she heard him whisper before turning away. She looked down at the photo, her hands shaking a little.

There it was, irrefutable. The crease had been digitally ironed out, showing clearly the tiny—no, the *infinitesimal* mark that was to be the downfall of Chantilly Dreams, the Gingerbread House and, in Greta's opinion anyway, the very heart and soul of the town of Spector.

"The Landmark Board will now adjourn to review these findings. We will notify all parties involved once a decision has been made." Somewhere inside, Greta was aware Patrick was speaking, but she couldn't take her eyes, her mind, off that horrible little mark in the photograph.

She barely heard Patrick as he banged the gavel, was barely aware of the Board standing and heading into the deliberation room to discuss her fate. She already knew how it would end.

Beside her, Jack touched her forearm, jarring her out of her shocked daze. "You know, I wouldn't put it past her to have doctored the document. It might behoove us to hire our own experts, refute the findings. It'll be expensive, though."

Great. More money.

Jack shook his head, reconsidering. "Then again, I'm sure their evidence would stand up to close scrutiny. She's got the money to pay for whatever she wants that damn document to say."

"And to pay the Honorable Mayor Cox whatever it took to see Winter's Haven become a reality," Greta mumbled. She shook her head in frustration, helpless tears filling her eyes.

Penny rushed up to her. "Oh please don't cry, Greta. We'll fight this. We'll get a hundred, no, a *thousand* people to stand in front of their blasted bulldozers."

Standing beside her, Penny's husband, Todd, the science teacher at the high school, cleared his throat. "Actually, hon, instead of a bulldozer, they'll probably use an excavator with hydraulic shears. See, they close the shears together to make a point. Like this."

He brought his fingers together to form a point, his eyes taking on an excited gleam as he stabbed at the air. "They pull down real hard and hopefully a big chunk of the house will rip away with it. Then they use the hydraulic shears to cut away the more stubborn parts." Now he made a scissors motion with his fingers, clawing away at his imaginary house. "And then . . ."

His voice trailed off when he saw that Penny had planted

one hand on her hip and was staring at him. "Are you done?"

A blush splotched across his cheeks. "Yeah." His eyes flicked over to Greta. "Jeez, I'm sorry, Greta."

"It's okay," Greta said. After all, she had to face it. She had thought she'd been handed a reprieve on a silver platter, but it had only been a cruel tease.

Ian Koslovsky caught her eye, and she saw the pity in his face. The room had quieted, and Greta glanced around to see everyone looking at her. So many familiar faces. Derek McClain, owner of one of Spector's two gas stations; Dotty Andrews, principal of the high school; Annie Clayton, manager of the Spector Inn; Jared Cliffe, Freddie Booker, Peter Woodward, Karen Simpson . . .

Greta saw the regret in all their expressions, even the ones who wanted the mall. Their faces blurred as tears again pooled in her eyes. She pressed them shut, but a trickle escaped and ran down her cheek.

It was over.

Chapter Six

His jaw clenched tight, Gray walked out of the town hall with Stephanie. She was downright jubilant but trying hard to keep it under wraps. After all, being happy about trouncing the underdog wouldn't look good PR-wise, would it?

Stephanie clutched his arm tighter and leaned into him. "You were brilliant in there," she gushed in a whisper. "Just brilliant."

Gray said nothing but began scanning the square for Greta. And then he spotted her off to the left with that attorney of hers, Jack Fenton, his arm supportively around her waist.

God, the look on her face, the desperation in her deep brown eyes. So defeated. So different from the way she had looked in her little shop—calm, confident, in control.

He had to talk to her, apologize, explain that he hadn't been in on the manipulative little publicity scheme Stephanie had hatched. "I'll be right back. I just want to . . ."

He'd been about to take a step, but Stephanie tugged on his arm, pulling him back. "Not now, darling. Give her a little time. I know you feel bad about all this." She laughed lightly. "I think it's actually really sweet of you."

Gray snorted out a breath. He didn't feel sweet.

Her eyes on Greta, Stephanie cocked her head, her smooth hair skimming across her shoulders. "To tell you the truth, I quite admire the intrepid Greta Kendall, fighting so very hard for something she believes in. We have that in common. Under different circumstances I could even see us becoming friends."

Gray cocked a brow at that but said nothing.

And maybe Stephanie was right. Greta might be more open to his apology a little later, after the shock had worn off. Although by then it might be too late, her mind already set on hating him. Torn by indecision, he stood there just watching Greta. She hadn't noticed him yet.

Overhead, the clouds shifted and the sun shone down once again, so intense at this altitude, instantly warming the air, making it feel more springlike. But he barely noticed the change in temperature.

He was absolutely amazed at what the sun had done to Greta's hair. Golden-red highlights caught the light and held it, the tumble of brown curls taking on a deep amber aura.

At that moment, Greta's gaze slid past Jack's shoulder, and she spotted him. He saw the warm brown of her eyes harden, darkening with anger, her mouth narrowing into a tight line. The anger completely transformed her face, and together with her brilliant hair, she became a force to be reckoned with.

Beside him, Stephanie squeezed his arm. "Grayson, did you hear me?" He tore his eyes away from Greta to look at Stephanie. "I said I made reservations at the Aspen Grill for six o'clock."

Gray let out a harsh chuckle. "What, a little victory dinner?"

Stephanie missed the ironic stab in the words. She gave him a quick smile, one that said she'd already moved past all this and now it was his turn to do so. "Absolutely."

She gently tugged on his arm in the direction of the street, and Gray allowed himself to be led away. As they headed over to her Escalade, he felt the cold prickles of Greta's stare on the back of his neck. He shivered despite the bright sun overhead.

Well, if she did decide to hate him, that was all right. The anger in her face had been infinitely better than the desperation.

And at least she had Fenton, her lawyer. It was obvious he cared for her. He was a good-looking kid, with that clean-cut, all-American thing he had going on. Straight out of a Ralph Lauren Polo ad. Except, of course, for that frayed jacket and those ill-fitting trousers. They pretty much screamed "student loans."

Gray let out a long, heavy breath as they crossed the street. "I'd like to stop by and see my dad on the way."

Stephanie flashed him a toothy smile as she fished around in her bag for her keys. "Oh, wonderful!"

He'd give her the benefit of the doubt on that one.

"So, how about a cup of coffee before I head back down the hill?" Jack asked. "We could discuss our game plan."

Greta tore her eyes from Gray and Stephanie walking toward the Escalade, where they were illegally parked in an alley across the street. Clearly, Stephanie Harwood was above any parking regulations. Where was a tow truck when you needed one?

Glancing up at Jack, Greta noted the shy hope in his eyes. Gosh, he was young. She wasn't sure exactly how old he was, but she'd bet mid-twenties, a good five years younger than she was. He'd passed the bar the year before, he'd told her, and hers was one of his first cases.

Not exactly an auspicious start.

She raised her eyebrows. "Do we *have* a game plan?"

"Well, no," Jack admitted with a sheepish grin that made him look even younger, almost a teenager. "Not yet."

"Thanks, but I think I'll just go back to the shop and open up again. This is a busy time of year for me, and I need the money. I've got some hefty lawyer bills to pay, you know." She tried for a teasing smile but apparently didn't quite manage it, as she saw his features crumple in dismay.

"I'm so sorry, Greta. I tried to get Harry to lower—"

"No, no, it's okay. I was only kidding. You and your firm did a great job. I'm happy to pay. Really." Even if it cost her the beloved 1971 Volkswagen Bug she'd had since college. There hadn't been too many choices by way of lawyers in Spector, so she'd had to opt for an Aspen firm. And anything Aspen was expensive.

Her gaze wandered back to Stephanie Harwood's Escalade just in time to see Gray lean in to kiss Stephanie good-bye through the open window. A fine, cold slice of anger stiffened Greta's spine, and she shook her head slowly, her eyes tracking Gray as he walked down the street toward his truck. "I just can't believe they're going to win. The fact that the government can take your house, your dreams, and turn them over to a money-grubbing developer . . ."

Jack shrugged in a mixture of sympathy and pragmatism. "We fought them off as well as we could, but we knew that part of it was a losing battle."

"I know, I know. The Supreme Court gave individual towns the power to set the balance between progress and preservation. Yada yada yada." Greta let out a bitter snort. "Except the blasted town council's blinded by dollar signs, champing at the bit to get their hands on all that money the mall will bring in. They don't give a hoot about preservation, especially Mayor Cox."

Jack touched her arm, his perfect features softening. "Look, don't give up yet. I don't have anything going on this afternoon. I'll go back to the office and start scouring the code again. Maybe I can find a loophole." He flashed her a wide smile. "Don't worry—it'll be off the clock. Pro bono."

"Thanks, Jack. I really appreciate it. I hope you find something."

She'd attempted some measure of optimism but knew she'd failed miserably.

Chapter Seven

Greta kept her eyes trained on the peppermint twist phlox her mother had planted along the brick path. They were just beginning to bloom their bright pink striped petals. In a couple of weeks there'd be two solid masses of them on either side of the path.

She still didn't look up as she approached the front steps. Even though she knew it was irrational, she simply couldn't face the house right now. She'd failed it. But not only the house; her grandparents, her mother.

"Mom?" Greta called as she walked inside and put her things down on the front counter. "Mom, I'm home." No cheery greeting met her in return. *Uh-oh.*

She checked Adele's workroom, but didn't find her there. A cool breeze wafted down the hallway from the kitchen. Oh no. Greta hurried down the hall and let out a gush of air. The back door was open!

"Mom!" Greta rushed outside and looked around the small backyard, and then spun around to check the side gate. It also stood open.

"Oh, Mom," she muttered and then ran through the gate and up along the side of the house to the front yard. A quick scan of the block in both directions proved fruitless.

Greta rushed back inside the house and grabbed her keys and purse. What was this, the fifth time her mother had wandered away? The first two times, she'd been only a couple of blocks away, walking with purpose and youthful energy, her mind firmly fixed in the past. The other times, Greta had found her at one of three familiar spots from her childhood, staring at places that no longer existed.

Greta jumped back in her Bug and zoomed down the street. First up what used to be a corner candy store five blocks away, now a dry cleaner. She stopped in front of the shop but saw no sign of her mother. Strike one.

She then drove three blocks south to St. Luke's, a beautiful Romanesque church built in 1891 during the height of the silver boom. Back in September, Greta had found her mother pulling on the doors, murmuring about being late for Sunday school. She jerked to a stop in front and ran inside.

It was empty. "Pastor Trane?" she called through the nave, and pastor Evan Trane stuck his head out from his small office to the right of the altar.

"Why, hello, Greta," he said, smiling, but he must have seen the anxiety on her face. "Something wrong?"

"Have you seen my mother?"

"I'm sorry, I haven't. Adele's wandered off again?"

"Looks like it."

"Would you like some help finding her?"

"No, thanks," Greta said, already heading back toward the door. "I've got one more place to try."

Strike two.

She drove a quarter mile back toward the edge of

town. It was far, but Adele could have made it. She'd had enough time.

At least it was a nice day, if a bit chilly. The bright sun overhead had burned away the last of the day's clouds. Only blue sky stretched over the valley Spector was nestled in, the mountain peaks on either side still white with snow, brilliant against the dazzling blue of the sky. The last time Adele had wandered away, it had been snowing, and she'd been wearing only her green housedress and a light sweater. She'd shivered for hours afterward despite the mug after mug of warmed apple cider Greta had handed her.

She turned onto the last road of the town, South Willow, drove a few hundred feet, and pulled over onto the side of the road.

There she was. Her mother was standing in the familiar meadow, surrounded by wildflowers and tall grasses, staring up at the single remaining chimney, a reminder of the house that had once been here before that terrible lightning storm so many years earlier. Greta turned the engine off, climbed out of the Bug, and crossed the road.

It was a wonderful piece of land, her family's favorite picnic spot throughout Greta's childhood. A little stream ran along the back of the property with graceful Aspen trees lining either side.

Adele spotted Greta as she approached, and she smiled a little girl's smile. "Hi, Aunt Ellen. I'm glad you're here. Did I come to the wrong place?"

Greta sighed. She knew she was the spitting image of her great-aunt. Adele had made the mistake before.

"Oh, Mom."

Suddenly it was all too much. Her house, her dear little

shop, her mother's sad condition. And then she was sobbing, her shoulders quaking uncontrollably.

Adele came over to her and touched her arm, a child comforting an adult. Greta slipped her arms around her, childishly wanting her mom, not the little girl she'd reverted back to. Adele hugged her back, and Greta welcomed the comfort, no longer caring who was holding her.

"Greta?" It was her mother's voice again, clear but confused. "Why . . . ?" Greta pulled back to smile at her mother through her tears. "I've been on one of my excursions, haven't I?"

"It's okay."

Her mother peered closely into Greta's face, her eyes suddenly awash in concern. "You're crying!"

Greta sniffled. "I'm fine. I'm just glad I found you. Now let's get you home."

They rode back together in silence until Greta turned onto their street. "It looks like we're in trouble with the house, Mom."

"What? Why? I thought—"

"I know, I did too. But we were wrong."

"But . . . our home."

"I know," Greta said again, her jaw tight, as she pulled up in front of the house and parked. For a moment they both sat there looking up at it, the gingerbread gleaming creamy white against the warm backdrop of brown. Greta had repainted just the summer before. Due to the hard winters at this altitude, the house needed repainting every six or seven years.

She'd never minded it, though. In fact, she'd always loved the ritual of it, those summers, the smell of the paint,

even the turpentine. As a little girl, she'd helped her grandfather and father, cleaning brushes, fetching lemonade,
and then she was thrilled as a teenager to be high on the
ladders scurrying up paint refills. And then it was just her
and her father. Now she did it alone, aided by a modern-day
paint sprayer.

The gingerbread took the longest, with all its nooks and
crannies, but Greta enjoyed every minute of it. She loved
the way the paint glistened fresh and new when she was
done.

With a sigh, she got out of the Bug and helped her
mother out. As she followed Adele up the path, Greta
glanced at the houses on either side. Like hers, they were
beautiful old Queen Annes, although not as well kept as
her house.

Also like hers, they'd both been businesses as well as
the owners' homes, a bookstore on the right, a pottery shop
on the left. But now they were like ghost houses, empty,
the owners happy to take the generous offers Harwood
Development had made them, happy for the "prime spots"
Stephanie had offered them in Winter's Haven.

Both were now slated for demolition—as hers also was
or soon would be. Hopefully Jack would be able to find
something, anything, to stop this from happening. She'd
seen the look in his eyes, though not a lot of hope there
despite his efforts to act otherwise. She felt bad for him.
He'd taken the case personally, perhaps too personally.

Greta unlocked the door, held it open for her mother,
and then checked the mailbox. Some ads and another lawyer bill. Perfect timing.

With a heavy sigh, Greta walked inside and set the bill

down next to the cash register. Once she sold her Bug, she'd have to figure out something for her mother's little forays into the past.

A bike maybe. Good thing they lived in a small town.

Chapter Eight

Maybe it wasn't the best time to visit his dad, clearly not one of his more lucid days. Absolutely no spark of recognition flickered in Henry Daniels' eyes when Gray and Stephanie walked into his dreary, dark room.

"Oh, Dad," Gray muttered in frustration. He headed across the room to draw back the heavy curtains. Through the window, the late afternoon sun shone just above the twin peaks of the Maroon Bells, brilliant pinks and grays already filling the sky. It would be a spectacular sunset.

The view was one of the reasons he'd picked this place. His father had always loved these mountains. But at the moment it seemed pointless. Henry didn't even glance at the view, but kept his eyes down on his hands, rubbing one thumb over the other, a fixed half smile on his face, his shoulders stiff, aware.

Gray knew this mode of his father's condition. His dad had no idea where he was or why, or who anyone else was. But rather than admit it, show his weakness, he acted like everything was fine. He knew what was going on. He was in control.

Gray sighed, and Stephanie squeezed his arm support-ively. This was the hardest to take. At least when Henry admitted he was lost in his mind, he could be cared for, consoled. But today it was all denials and smiles.

Gray was already in a rotten mood, and though he tried to hide it, it seemed to resonate with his dad's agitation and only increased it. Henry began rubbing his thumb harder against the other, the skin below the nail reddening.

"Honey, I think it's time to go," Stephanie whispered in his ear, her eyes on Henry.

"What are you two whispering about over there?" Henry barked, his brows furrowed in sharp suspicion.

"Nothing, Dad," Gray said quickly. "I think we're just going to go for now, okay? But we'll stop by again soon."

Henry seemed to instantly calm down at the prospect of their leaving, and that thought formed a lump in Gray's throat that made it hurt to swallow.

"Fine, then, nice to see you." Henry gave them a dismissive little wave. He still had no idea who these strangers were, and now he just wanted them gone.

"Come on, honey," Stephanie said gently and led Gray out of the room.

Gray glanced back just as he was heading out the door and caught sight of his dad's face. Now with no need for a false front, Gray saw the haunted desperation there, the bewilderment. As the sun glinted off tears welling in his father's eyes, Gray let out a long, slow breath.

The Aspen Grill's excellent beef Wellington was wasted on Gray that night, his stomach tight and uncomfortable. A heavy stone of guilt had settled in there but good. Guilt at checking his father into that place, guilt over what happened today in that horrible landmark meeting.

Stephanie was sweet, trying to distract him with talk about the wedding and their new house in Aspen, not mentioning Winter's Haven even once. Definitely not the norm for her. That blasted mall had been Topic Number One for a solid year. But not tonight.

She even let him drink two Manhattans as opposed to his usual one, offering to drive him home. Thanks to the alcohol, Gray had dropped quickly off to sleep, but he awoke at two and never really got back to sleep for the rest of the night.

He looked over at the digital clock beside the bed: 5:04. Closing his eyes, he tried to blank out his brain for sleep, but immediately the thoughts began whirling, about what had happened that day, what he had done to Greta Kendall, what she must think of him.

For the hundredth time that night, her expression outside the town hall came to him vividly, the lost, miserable look in her eyes, the hope of saving her house all but gone. And on the heels of that, how she'd looked after catching sight of him, her brown eyes, so warm and friendly the first time he'd come into the store, narrowing into thin slits of pure fury. Fierce. Sexy.

All right, there it was. She'd looked incredibly sexy standing there, hadn't she? The afternoon sun gleaming in her hair, her shoulders raised, tense, a cat ready to pounce. Was it okay to find another woman that sexy a few weeks before your wedding? He'd have to think about that.

A rustling noise came from the attic as the squirrels up there began stirring.

"Morning, guys," Gray murmured, and having given up on any more sleep, he lumbered out of bed to face the day.

Chapter Nine

Late the next morning, Greta began restocking her selection of blue garters for the last time. She'd be doing a
lot of things for the last time, wouldn't she?

The bell over the door tinkled, and in walked Gray
Daniels wearing jeans and a dark gray T-shirt.

Her heart fluttered, just a little, but still undeniably.
What was that about? She should be angry, furious at the
sight of him. *Focus.*

Standing, Greta brushed bits of Styrofoam peanuts off
her skirt while working to set her face as mean and hard
as she could.

Gray walked toward her and stopped a good ten feet
away. Maybe her menacing act had worked. He definitely
looked uncomfortable, clearly unable to decide what to do
with his hands. He ended up jamming them in the pockets
of his jeans. "I just wanted to say how sorry I am about
what happened yesterday."

Greta set her jaw. "Fine, you're sorry. I get it."

She turned back to the garters, but she knew he wouldn't
be satisfied with that. Why was she dragging this out? She
should just tell him to get the heck out of her store and
be done with it.

She felt a touch at her arm. "Please, can I explain?"

That triggered her anger. Finally.

She spun around to face him as a tide of real fury swept over her. "What is there to explain? You—*you personally*—just pulled the rug that was my home, my livelihood, out from under me and my mother."

"I know, but—"

"What do you want from me?" Greta demanded, planting her hands on her hips. "Absolution? Well, I suggest you go to St. Luke's across town for that. I'm not offering any."

The stiff discomfort in his face softened, his eyes now imploring. "Would you believe me if I told you I didn't know what she was planning here yesterday? I didn't know this was the site of her blasted mall."

Greta scoffed. "How could you not know?" It had been all over the papers the last year and then some.

Gray shrugged, quick and hard. "I've been down at my dad's place in Aspen."

Not good enough. "It's been in both the *Aspen Times* and the *Daily News*." They'd both interviewed her the month before. The mall was big news in Pitkin County.

"I haven't touched a paper in months. I've been taking care of my dad twenty-four/seven."

Greta huffed out a scornful breath. "What, a future Harwood can't afford a full-time nurse?"

Gray shook his head. "After he fired the last one, the agency didn't send out any more. They said he was abusive. He's not, though. He's a kind, gentle man. He just gets so confused now and then he gets angry and lashes out at anything and everyone around him." As Gray raised his palms, pleading, Greta felt the hardness in her heart begin to dislodge. "But he's just scared. You should have seen him. He looked so helpless, so desperate in that room."

His gaze skittered away from her toward the window, and Greta saw his chin quiver. "When I left him yesterday, he was crying." Gray's voice broke on the last word, his shoulders quaking in a sudden sob. Greta felt the last of her anger crumble away, compassion taking over. He flashed her an embarrassed smile through his tears. "Sorry. Like father, like son, huh?"

Greta went over to the counter, grabbed a tissue from the shelf under the register and brought it over to him.

As he wiped his eyes, Greta saw in them the devastation she'd seen in her own eyes after one of her mother's bad days. She took a step toward him and touched his forearm.

"You know what I think? I think it's a natural process. Beyond your, *our*, control. Accept that and concentrate on what you *can* control. Nurture their happy moments and make them as comfortable as you can, until you need help doing that. You did that, right? I'll bet you researched every nursing home in the county."

Gray nodded and again managed a small smile. "I did look out a lot of windows. I wanted him to have a nice view."

Greta grinned. "See? You did your best. It's all you can do." Without even thinking about it, she slipped her hand down from his forearm to his hand and squeezed it. He squeezed hers back, and Greta could feel his desperation.

She looked up into his eyes, saw them trained on hers. He was no longer smiling.

For a moment they just stood there, their eyes locked. He seemed to become aware of himself then, of her, and something shifted in the way he was looking at her, becoming soft, tender. His gaze left her eyes and moved around her face, really *seeing* her, taking her in.

She'd seen that look in other men's eyes, in Jack Fenton's eyes. A man looking at a woman he'd just begun to have feelings for. And with a shock, she realized she was looking at Gray Daniels in exactly the same way.

His gaze made its way back to her eyes, and for a moment they just stood there, their breaths quick and shallow, both waiting for something neither wanted to think about.

A horn blasted from outside. Loud, sustained. Stephanie. In unison, their eyes cut toward the window, their hands coming apart.

Gray blinked several times, drew in a sharp breath, and let it out in a rush before turning back to Greta. "I'd better go. And look, I really am sorry. If I'd known what she was up to, I never would have allowed it."

At that, Greta couldn't help a quick, wry smile from springing to her lips. "Really. I don't think a freight train could stop that woman when she wants something. But you would know better about that, wouldn't you?"

She heard the bitter tinge in her voice and realized her anger was sparking up again, the sympathy she'd felt for him a moment earlier—and whatever *else* that had been— beginning to dissipate.

Gray cleared his throat and looked increasingly uncomfortable standing there.

Greta cocked her head. "Is there something else I can do for you?" A clear bite of anger came through the words, and Gray winced.

"My grandmother's dress . . ."

Darn, she'd forgotten all about that. She strode to the back of the store and looked into her mother's workroom.

Adele was busily working on the Mainbocher, sewing a restored string of beads onto the bodice while humming a familiar little melody.

For a moment, Greta just watched her from the door, basking in the contented glow her mother was radiating.

"'Nurture happy moments,' remember?" Gray murmured, suddenly beside her. "Why don't we let her finish it? I'll be glad to pay, no matter the cost."

Greta tore her eyes away from her mother to give him a cool smile. "Oh, yeah?" She headed over to the counter and picked up the envelope she hadn't touched since yesterday, not wanting to see what the latest acts of futility had cost in her war with Harwood Development.

She slid her finger across the top and pulled out the bill. "How about three thousand, two hundred four dollars and sixty-one cents?" Gray raised his eyebrows in surprise. "'Spare no expense,' remember? Don't forget, you're going to be a Harwood soon. You need to act the part."

Shame slid into Gray's eyes, and he looked away from her, raking a hand through his hair, making one side stand straight up before gravity pulled it back down into place.

Another honk quickly followed by a second and third from the Escalade.

"Fine then," he said gruffly and pulled his wallet out from his jacket. He took out a business card and handed it to her. J. P. STEPHENS, ATTORNEYS AT LAW. "I'm not with them anymore, but my cell's on there. Call me when you're done."

Another honk came and he was gone.

From behind her, Greta heard her cell phone vibrating against the counter by the cash register. She walked over to it and glanced down at the caller ID. Jack Fenton. She grabbed the phone, her heart thumping.

"Hi, Jack, did you find anything?"

A sigh came through the line. "Sorry, I didn't. The code's sealed up pretty tight. There's nothing more we can do. We've already explored every possibility, filed as many protests as we could, got all the required signatures, forced every conceivable hearing."

Greta felt her heart constrict painfully in her chest. She walked over to the window seat her grandfather had built and sat down. As a child she'd spent many Saturday afternoons right here, soaking in the warm bright sunlight of spring while happy brides shopped all around her.

The flowery pattern on the cushion blurred together as tears welled in her eyes.

"I'm so sorry, Greta."

"Me too." A lump forming in her throat made it hard to talk. "Thanks, Jack," she managed, and hung up.

The bell tinkled, and her three o'clock appointment came in, a young bride named Audrey, ready to try on dresses for the best day of her life.

Greta swallowed hard, and the lump diminished but didn't go away completely. She suspected it would be around for a while.

Brushing her tears away, she stood up and somehow pulled a smile together. Still, it felt forced and unnatural.

Luckily, the bride was so excited she didn't notice.

Chapter Ten

The next day Greta allowed herself an extra hour of rest in the morning. She'd had a bad night, alternating between troubled, fretful sleep and stark periods of wakefulness, the reality of the situation fully sinking in.

She'd lost her little war, hadn't she? As Jack had made clear, there were no more battlefields on which to fight. Time to face facts.

Fact Number One: she'd better start looking for a temporary place for her and her mother to stay. Also some storage space for all her merchandise until she could figure out what to do.

Glad to have an activity, she opened the front door and bent down to get the paper. Ian Koslovsky listed all the available apartments in Spector on the back page. There were never very many, but hopefully she'd find something nice. She hated the idea of her mother moving from the Gingerbread House into some cheap little apartment, even if it was only temporary.

Greta was turning to go back inside when she saw something sticking out of the mailbox, a manila envelope. She frowned. It was too early for the mail. Curious, she pulled it out of the box. Her heartbeat quickened when she saw the neatly typed label with her name and address but no return address or postage. Another gift from her new "friend"?

She slipped her finger under the flap and ripped it open. Inside was an old photograph of her house, one she'd never seen before. Funny, she'd thought she had all the early pictures of her house, each one proudly hung on the wall in the foyer.

In this photo, a young man stood on the top step, one foot on the porch, his back straight and proud. In front of the door stood a pretty, petite woman, a girl in braids around ten years old to her right, and a younger boy to her left. A girl about five years old clung shyly to her mother's skirts.

CLEMENS FAMILY—JUNE 1893 was printed across the bottom of the photo. Paper-clipped to the photo was a note, written in the same tilted handwriting as before.

Ms. Kendall,

I'm sorry my previous attempt at helping you save your house proved so fruitless. However, further re-search into the history of your house has produced another item that may yield better results.

As you probably know, your house was built in 1889 by a silver miner named Zachary Clemens. When the Sherman Silver Purchase Act was re-pealed in 1893, he was ruined, as were many miners and mining companies in the area. In order to pro-vide for his wife and three young children, he took a job as the postmaster for Spector. Note the small sign in the window on the left side of the photo.

Greta flipped back to the photo and focused in on the sign in the window. She could just make out the handwritten block letters, POST OFFICE, SPECTOR, COLORADO.

She turned back to the note.

According to my research, your house was the site of the first official post office above ten thousand feet. It should therefore meet the criteria for landmark status.

Good luck!

—*A friend*

Greta grinned. "There's your battlefield, Jack."

She heard a car door slam and looked up to see Gray Daniels in his truck parked across the street. She frowned. Gray was her mysterious benefactor? But he was the one who'd defeated her in court with the birth certificate!

Then again, maybe he hadn't known. When he had sneaked it into her mailbox, he may have had every reason to believe the address on it was hers. In fact, he'd probably been just as surprised as she when the 1 was shown to actually be a 7.

And here he was helping her again.

"Hey!" she yelled out, heading over to him.

Gray looked up, startled, as she approached the truck. He rolled down the window.

"Thank you so much," Greta said, beaming.

She was surprised to see only wariness in his blue eyes. "Look, I said I was sorry."

Greta nodded. "I see that now. Would you like to come in for some coffee?"

"No, thanks. I've got to get going."

From behind her, Greta heard her mother's voice. "Pancakes are ready, Greta! Maybe your friend would like some too? There's plenty."

"Thanks, Mom!" She turned back to Gray as her mother ducked back inside the house. "How about it? My mother makes the best gingerbread pancakes on the planet, *and* we have real maple syrup from my cousin in Vermont." Gray seemed to hesitate. "Come on. It's the least we can do."

His forehead creased. "For what?"

Greta laughed. "Okay, okay, I get it. Keep it on the down-low. Done. Now come on—it's pancake time."

Gray's pretended confusion dissolved into a tentative smile. "I do like a good pancake."

"Best on the planet, I'm telling you."

"All right, then, how can I resist?"

He climbed out of his truck, and together they headed back to the house.

Chapter Eleven

One more?" Adele asked, a pancake poised on her spatula above Gray's plate.

Gray shook his head adamantly and sat back in his chair, patting his belly. "No, thanks. I'm stuffed to the gills." He smiled over at Greta. "And you're right. *The* most delicious pancakes I've ever had."

Gray spotted the blush spreading across Adele's cheeks as she set the pancake back down on the warming plate. "Oh, you're just saying that."

"No, ma'am," Gray said, shaking his head. "Best on the planet, just like Greta said." Clearly pleased, Adele sat down and took a sip of tea. "And how perfectly appropriate to be eating gingerbread pancakes in a gingerbread house."

At that, Adele flashed a smile at Greta. "Did you tell him about your name?"

Greta groaned. "Oh, please, Mom, no."

Intrigued, Gray sat up straighter. "What? Wait, don't tell me. Let me guess." He sat back again and gave Greta an appraising look. "Let's see, *Greta . . .*" He raised his eyebrows at Adele. "You were a big Garbo fan?"

Adele chuckled. "No."

"What then?"

Adele nodded at Greta. "You tell him."

Greta heaved out a resigned breath. "Fine then. It's actually short for Gretel, as in Hansel and . . . ?"

"As in Gingerbread House," Gray said, laughing. "Got it. Cute."

Greta rolled her eyes. "Thanks." She gave her mother a fond smile. "My grandfather painted the house this way for my mom when she was a little girl, and ever since then she's lived in something of a storybook land."

Adele let out a huff. "And what's so wrong with that? Real life can be so very . . . brutal." Her smile fading, she reached over and squeezed Greta's hand. "Well, I'd better get started on the dishes." She got up and headed over to the sink.

Greta glanced at Gray and must have seen the question in his eyes. "My ex."

Gray drew in a quick rush of air. "Gosh, Greta, I'm so sorry."

But Greta shrugged as if it were no big deal, although clearly it had been. He noticed she was rubbing her wrist between her thumb and index finger. "It's done with."

Is it? The thought automatically sprang to Gray's mind as something old and deeply ingrained crept into Greta's eyes, haunting them.

Her jaw set, Greta rose. "I'll do those, Mom."

Gray watched as Greta headed over to her mother, his stomach tight with anger. Anger at the man who had hurt her. But then shame slipped right in next to the anger. *He'd* hurt her, hadn't he? Even though she'd seemed to have forgiven him, undeniably a load off his heart. Still, it was a little baffling, wasn't it? Welcoming him into the home he'd helped doom, serving him breakfast? As nice as she and her mother had been to him, he wouldn't be surprised if he dropped dead in two hours from eating pancakes laced with poison.

Despite Adele's protests, Greta gently pulled her away from the sink. "Why don't you go and get started on the dress?"

Adele nodded. "Yes, all right." Turning, she beamed at Gray. "It's going to be so beautiful. Your bride will look absolutely gorgeous."

Gray returned her smile even though he suddenly felt a little awkward. "I'm sure she will."

As Adele headed out of the room Gray walked over to Greta and nodded down at the dishes stacked in the sink. "Need any help with those?"

"No, thanks, I'm fine," Greta said, squeezing some dish-washing soap into the rising water.

"All right, then, I'd better get going. Stephanie's probably wondering where I am. We're taste testing cakes today."

"Oh," Greta said, and something in her voice made Gray pause. She turned the water off and pivoted around slowly, wiping her hands on a kitchen towel. Training her brown eyes on him, she held him in an intent, curious gaze that made him feel acutely self-conscious.

"What?" he asked and heard the defensiveness in the word.

Greta raised one shoulder in a half shrug. "I don't know. You seem like such a nice guy. And she's . . . not."

Gray nodded. He couldn't blame her for feeling that way. "Let's just say we've known each other for a very long time. There's a lot more to her than what you've seen."

Again, Greta shrugged. "If you say so."

Gray studied her for a long moment, her shoulders tense, her eyes on the kitchen towel she was twisting in her hands. "She admires you, you know."

Greta jerked her head up to look right at him, brows raised in surprise.

He nodded. "For fighting so hard for what you believe in. She says you have that in common."

Greta let out a light snort. "She *believes* in a mall?"

"No, what she's really fighting for is her father's respect."

Greta cocked her head at him. "And the only way to that is through my house?"

Gray lifted his shoulders in a pragmatic shrug. "In her mind, yes."

Greta said nothing, but Gray saw a muscle twitch in her jaw. He felt suddenly uncomfortable, the cozy kitchen closing in on him. "Well, I should go." His voice sounded a little more gruff than he'd intended. He forced a smile. "Thanks for breakfast."

Her return smile looked as stiff as his felt. "Sure. Come on—I'll walk you out."

As they passed by Adele's workroom, Gray stopped. "Thanks for the pancakes, Adele. They really were the best I've ever had."

"Anytime," Adele sang out as another blush tickled her cheeks. She was sitting beside the Mainbocher's dress form, threading a needle.

Gray's eyes shifted to the dress. It looked a little shabby hanging there, didn't it? So different from the wedding-day photos taken of his mother and grandmother, the dress glorious in the sunlight, the beads gleaming like tiny diamonds.

Adele must have seen the doubt on his face. "Don't worry, it'll be perfect once we're through with it. Good as new. I promise."

"Thanks. I really appreciate your taking it on."

"Oh, but it's an honor! Mainbocher has always been a favorite designer of mine. You know, he designed Wallis Simpson's wedding dress when she married King Edward VIII." Her brown eyes gleamed. "He abdicated the throne just to marry her, a divorced American who wouldn't have been accepted as queen. Isn't that romantic?"

"It sure is," Gray said, nodding. "Love can be a powerful motivator."

"Love schmove," Greta muttered beside him. "It was no secret Edward hated being king. I bet he just jumped at the chance to get out of it."

Adele shook her head, her eyes sad as she looked at her daughter. "Oh, Greta."

Gray agreed. He wondered if her ex was to blame for her cynicism.

Greta touched his arm. "Come on, you'd better get going. We wouldn't want to keep your Stephanie waiting now, would we?"

The second the words were out of her mouth, Greta cringed. "I'm sorry. That was rude."

"No, I get it," Gray said, as they headed through the shop toward the door. "I'm sure she's not exactly your favorite person in the world at the moment."

Greta gave him a little half smile of acknowledgment. "Not exactly. But I didn't mean to take it out on you."

Gray lifted one shoulder in a quick shrug. "That's okay." He pulled his keys out from his pocket. "Well, thanks again for breakfast."

"No, Gray," Greta said, shaking her head as she touched his arm again. "Thank *you*." She winked so it would be clear she was no longer talking about pancakes.

He frowned, pretending to be baffled. "For what exactly?"

Greta let out a little laugh and then nodded, affecting a suddenly stern expression. "Right, right. Nothing." She swept her thumb and index finger across her mouth in a zipping gesture. "Consider them sealed."

"Okay," Gray said slowly, still looking completely confused. He was quite the actor, wasn't he?

"Oh, and my mom makes pancakes every Saturday. You're more than welcome to stop by and . . ."

She stopped when Gray started shaking his head. "Thanks, but I . . . I can't."

"Why not?"

Gray took a step closer to her, intimately close, his eyes boring into hers, the blue in them darkening to near black. "You know why." His voice was low and the huskiness in it sent a small thrill shooting through her stomach. "Goodbye, Greta." Gray turned and headed for his truck.

Greta just stood there, watching him, her belly still tingling. That was bad. Her feelings for him weren't going away, were they? That heady rush of attraction was only getting stronger every time she saw him. And it had lingered all the way through breakfast.

What an unexpectedly wonderful time that had been. He'd fit right in with her and her mom. The conversation had sparkled with energy, wit, and humor. He had such a marvelous natural smile, fully at ease with himself and his surroundings.

Several times she caught herself staring at him as she'd become fixated on just one part of his face, his mouth of course, with those full strong lips, but also his cheekbones, his chin, his perfect little nose. Mostly though, she'd been caught up in his eyes, the blue of them shifting between light and dark, as if being teased by a sunbeam coming down through a treetop.

Greta burst out a wry laugh at that. *Really? Sunbeams and treetops?* She shook her head as she closed the front door and leaned against it.

Yes, really.

Chapter Twelve

As she waited for the special session of the landmark board to begin, Greta found herself scanning the crowded room for Gray Daniels. He was nowhere in sight. She understood completely. He'd gone behind his fiancée's back, supplying Greta with evidence that would save her house.

Still, she would have loved the opportunity to thank him one more time, even if it was just by way of a quick wink on the sly. Oh, but who was she fooling? She just wanted to see *him*.

Stop it, she scolded herself.

Of course Stephanie Harwood was there, parked as usual at the table on the opposite side. For once, they were both alone. Jack Fenton hadn't come, trying to save Greta some money. He'd generously offered to explain how to file all the paperwork herself.

Patrick Shaw banged his gavel several times, quieting the raucous crowd. He smiled down at Greta. "Well, we've been here before, haven't we, Ms. Kendall?"

Greta grinned. "Yes, we have, Chairman Shaw."

She knew by his smile that the board had decided in her favor after reviewing the photo Gray had given her. Thank God. Maybe this ordeal was at last truly over.

She caught movement in the corner of her eye and looked over to see Gray slip onto the bench behind Stephanie. He was frowning, his jaw set. Did Stephanie find out what he'd done? Greta glanced at her. She didn't look angry. Instead, she had that news-anchor smile plastered on her lips. Hiding her fury?

Greta's gaze trailed back to Gray, and she blinked as she saw him looking directly at her. He wasn't smiling, his mouth a thin line. He seemed to be trying to convey something to her with his eyes. A warning? Oh, no. Not again.

"Well, Ms. Kendall," Patrick began, "the board has examined the new evidence you've acquired, and we unanimously agree that it more than meets the criteria for landmark status. We therefore—"

"Excuse me, Mr. Chairman," Stephanie Harwood said, rising to her feet. "I am here to protest granting landmark status to the property in question."

As Greta watched Stephanie raise a photograph high in the air, an uncomfortable feeling of déjà vu began to set in. This hadn't ended well the last time.

"I have here a photograph of a building located in Willowby, Colorado, altitude 10,302 feet. Note the sign above the door: POST OFFICE."

From her table, Greta could see it was an old photo of a simple single-story building standing alone. Stephanie raised another picture. "Here is another photograph showing the same structure with a new building now beside it. The date of the second building's construction is clearly visible above the door: 1891."

Behind them the crowd burst out into hushed excited

whispers. Patrick banged his gavel again. "Please continue, Ms. Harwood." He was no longer smiling.

Stephanie cleared her throat before resuming. "Although the original structure is now gone, these photographs indeed prove the existence of a post office above ten thousand feet at least two years earlier than Ms. Kendall's house."

Walking up to the platform, she handed a set of both photographs to each board member, and then headed over to Greta. "I'm sorry," she said in a low voice as she handed her the photos. "This isn't personal. I hope you know that."

Greta was so taken aback by the simple sincerity in Stephanie's eyes that she said nothing, only sat staring numbly after her as she walked backed to her table.

Patrick examined the photos closely and then waved the other board members together. As they leaned in, he covered the microphone with his hand. They conferred for a moment, and Greta watched their faces. She saw the grimness set in and felt her stomach clench tight.

At last, they all leaned back in their seats, and Patrick pulled the microphone toward him. He let out a long sigh before speaking. "The board accepts the submission of this new evidence and will now adjourn to review it." He turned to Greta. "Ms. Kendall, would you like time to hire your own expert to examine this evidence?"

She could see from his eyes that he wanted her to. But Jack was right. If Stephanie had in fact doctored the photo, she would have made certain it would pass muster. It would be like throwing money away, money she didn't have.

She shook her head and began to speak, but found her

throat had closed up tight. She swallowed hard and felt it let up a little. "No, Mr. Chairman."

"Very well then. We will notify you when we've reached a decision in this matter." He adjourned the meeting and headed into the deliberation room with the rest of the board, none of them smiling.

Greta let the two photos flutter down onto the table and sat back in her chair. She bit the inside of her lip, willing herself not to cry. A squeeze at her elbow startled her, and she turned to see Ian Koslovsky leaning forward from the bench behind her. "I'm so sorry, Greta."

Again, she could only nod. The feeling of déjà vu returned as she looked beyond him and saw the people of Spector once again relaying intense sympathy with their eyes.

This time, though, instead of being overwhelmed by defeat and helplessness, anger took over. Anger aimed directly at that man across the aisle.

Greta grabbed her purse and marched right over there. Spotting her, Stephanie stood up, her back rigid, ready for a confrontation. She looked surprised when Greta instead rounded on Gray.

"Why did you give me that note? If you knew it wasn't true, why did you even bother? Are you *trying* to torture me?"

"Gray?" Stephanie said, looking at them in confusion. "What's she talking about?"

"I have no idea," he said, his voice low and gruff, his eyes still on Greta.

She cocked an eyebrow at him. "Really. The note? The picture? My mailbox?"

But she saw only genuine bewilderment in his dark eyes. She let out a breath. It hadn't been him. Whoever "a friend" was, it wasn't Gray Daniels.

"Never mind," she muttered, swinging her purse strap up over her shoulder. "Obviously, I was wrong about you. You're definitely no friend of mine."

With that, she walked down the center aisle, her eyes on the floor ahead of her, avoiding the stifling pity she knew would surround her yet again.

Chapter Thirteen

Greta grabbed another cardboard box from the stack in the middle of the room, folded together the bottom flaps, and ran the packing tape across it twice. She was getting good at this.

She didn't want to be good at this.

At least it was nearly done. She was packing up her room, her beloved peach and ivory room, which would soon be no more.

As a little girl Greta had felt like such a princess living here. She'd pretend the turret was a tower and she was Rapunzel or Sleeping Beauty.

Straightening, Greta pressed her knuckles against her spine, trying to relax the aching muscles there. Time for a break.

She headed over to her favorite part of the room, a corner nook rounded by the turret, and collapsed on the chaise longue her father had built for her. Her mother had upholstered it in a creamy peach, with ivory fringe dangling from the sides. The matching pillows had already been packed away.

Greta breathed out probably her hundredth sigh of the morning. She'd spent countless afternoons lying here reading, fairy tales at first, later romance novels and mysteries as she grew older. So many happy memories. She allowed herself to indulge in them for just a little while before hauling herself back off the chaise.

Time was growing short, and she and her mother still had a lifetime of things to pack. Already they'd thrown away dozens of trash bags and boxes full of useless stuff. No doubt much of it would have been purged during some move or another, but her mother had lived here since she was ten years old. Stuff had a way of accumulating over that amount of time. And accumulate it had. So much to sort through and decide the fate over.

It was especially hard on her mother, who had found herself basically evicted from her own life. Greta had tried to see the positive in all this, but so far she hadn't come up with much. Then again, sometimes life just threw you curveballs, and you simply had to roll with the punches.

Greta grinned. Talk about mixing metaphors. Well, at least she could find some humor in it. That was something, right?

Steeling herself, she picked up a piece of cardboard and assembled yet another box.

A half hour later, Greta jumped, startled by something large and metallic crashing to the ground outside, followed by a thunderous yet oddly hollow noise.

She looked out the window and saw a semi pulling away after dropping off an enormous Dumpster next door, in front of what used to be her neighbor Jill's quaint little bookstore. DREW'S DEMOLITION was stenciled on the side of the Dumpster in block letters.

A bright orange excavator was rumbling off the platform

of another truck, guided by two workmen wearing hard-hats and Day-Glo vests. So Penny's husband had been right. Not a bulldozer in sight.

The machine lumbered up to and over the curb, breaking off pieces of it, bits of concrete crumbling into the street. No one seemed to care. And really, why should they? In a few short months, this entire area would probably be a parking lot for Winter's Haven.

One of the workmen let out a shrill whistle, and the excavator paused, its smokestack jetting out a puff of black as the workman climbed up to the cab to talk to the driver. Greta could hear him shout something indiscernible above the clamor of the motor. The driver nodded and the workman jumped back down. He and the other workmen stepped back a few feet.

For a moment the excavator remained still, the engine idling as the driver seemed to contemplate his best plan of attack. Suddenly it burst into life, bellowing out what sounded very much to Greta like an ominous roar. Then it was charging forward, hurtling toward Jill's house.

It lurched to a stop a few feet in front of it, and the massive metal claw began unfurling, Todd's hydraulic shears attached to the end of it. Exactly as he'd described, the shears slammed shut with an enormous clang, forming a menacing point.

Without hesitation, the driver raised the claw and brought it down hard, punching right through the roof of the front porch and then, sawing back and forth, pulling away half the roof with it. Even through the thick glass of the window, Greta heard the wood creak and then crack, shrieking as it ripped apart.

She pressed her hand against her chest, tears welling in her eyes. The house sounded like it was screaming out in pain!

The excavator reared back, veered a few feet to the right, and then the claw was swinging up and back down again, mercilessly slashing into what remained of the porch roof.

Part of the turret split off and came away with it, the bay windows shattering, sending century-old glass trickling down to the ground like a terrible waterfall.

Greta caught a glimpse of cheery yellow and realized it was the upholstery from a window seat Jill had built along the inside of the turret, creating a cozy little reading area for her customers.

As the excavator jerked back for yet another run, Greta burst out a sob and closed her eyes, unable to bear it a moment longer. It was just so . . . ruthless.

She turned away from the window and opened her eyes to see her mother standing at the other window, tears silently streaming down her face, her shoulders quaking. With all the racket from outside, Greta hadn't heard her come in.

No way did her mother need to watch this.

"Oh, Mom, don't look at that." Sniffling, Greta put her arm around her mother's waist and pulled her away from the window. "I'll come and help you in your room for a while."

It was on the other side of the house, and Greta wanted to get her mother as far away as possible from that horrible machine.

Chapter Fourteen

Greta carefully set her mother's antique alarm clock in the moving box, along with the other last-minute things. The movers had gotten everything else the day before.

Unfortunately, Greta had seriously overestimated the size of the new apartment. By the time everything was stuffed in there, it had been nearly impossible to even walk around. She'd have to put a lot more in storage. Exhausted, both emotionally and physically, she and her mother had opted to spend one last night in the house.

Greta was fine with a sleeping bag, but she couldn't have her mother sleeping on the floor. Instead, she'd had the three buff college students she'd hired bring her mother's mattress back to the house and set it up in the front room.

She hefted up the last box and headed out the door. It wasn't very heavy, but it was bulky and unwieldy, and she had to keep jostling it around just to maintain her grip.

"Need some help with that?"

Greta peered around the side of the box and saw Gray Daniels leaning against his truck, parked next door. Like her, he was wearing shorts and a T-shirt, taking advantage of the unusually warm day.

But what the heck was he doing here? Maybe he really

did enjoy torturing her, watching with sadistic glee as she was forced out of her beloved home.

"No, thanks," she said, keeping her voice low and as unfriendly as possible. "I got it."

He shrugged and began writing something on a clip-board.

Greta made it to her car and somehow got the door opened. She tried to squeeze the box into the backseat of the Bug, but the corners wouldn't clear the space behind the passenger seat, even though it was pushed forward as far as it would go.

Balancing the box precariously on her knee, Greta yanked the seat back and jammed the box into the passenger's side. It filled the seat completely, but that was all right. Her mother was at the new apartment, setting up her makeshift workroom.

Greta slammed the door closed, jarring the box, but the door remained shut. She huffed away a strand of hair that had fallen out of her ponytail and glanced over at Gray, who was busily jotting down notes.

Curiosity won out. "What are you doing here, anyway?" It sounded abrasive and demanding and she didn't care.

"Just taking some more measurements," Gray said, his eyes still on his notes. "Trueing up the specs on the original drawings."

Greta frowned. "I thought you were a lawyer."

Now he did glance over at her, a slight smile curling his lips. "That's right, I *was* a lawyer. I'm out of that game. Now I'm going to be an architect."

Greta felt her mouth twitch. He may as well have been five years old, standing there declaring "I'm going to be an astronaut!" He sounded so proud and excited. Still, she wouldn't allow herself to smile at him.

"Well, that's quite a switch."

He shrugged. "I'm not too big on conflict, and there was a lot of that in the law business."

"Ah." Feeling no need to say anything further, Greta headed back inside the house.

Only the mattress to go. It was queen-size and heavy, but she thought she could manage it. She still had the flat dolly the storage place had lent her.

Heaving the mattress up onto its side, she leaned it against the wall and then brought the dolly over. She jerked up one corner, pulling the dolly in under it with her foot. She went around to the other side, hoisted up the other corner, and shimmied it too onto the dolly. So far so good.

Rolling it toward the door, she struggled to balance the mattress as it swayed back and forth. She figured once she got to the Bug, she could just let it fall across the roof and then tie it down with bungee cords. She didn't need to go far, only a few blocks over to where she'd found a cute if shabby little apartment in an adobe-style building.

Now if she could only wrestle the thing down the porch steps. She bumped the dolly over the threshold of the front door and out onto the porch. She thought she could slide the mattress down the stairs vertically, assuming she could control the fall from the side.

Unfortunately, once the mattress tilted past the first step, gravity had its way with it, and the mattress careened down the stairs, wobbling wildly from side to side.

Letting out a little scream, Greta jumped down the last

couple of steps and tried to get out of the way, but as one corner of the mattress struck the ground, it bounced up and came crashing down right on top of her, knocking her flat. Fortunately, the thick pink carpet of peppermint twist phlox cushioned her fall.

For a moment she just lay there under the beast, breathing hard. Okay, new plan. Item One: get the blasted thing off her. She shoved hard against it, but it was heavy and her muscles were tired from moving boxes all day yesterday. Oh, but maybe Gray was still around. It was a humiliating prospect, yet—

In that moment, the weight of the mattress suddenly eased as it was pulled up and off her.

"Are you okay?" Gray asked, holding the sides of the mattress firmly as he looked down at her in concern.

"I'm fine," Greta mumbled, her cheeks hot and itchy as she got to her feet. She brushed crushed phlox petals off her shorts and T-shirt. "Thanks."

Gray nodded and lifted up the mattress effortlessly. "I'll just throw it in the back of my truck."

Without waiting for her response, he began hauling the mattress down the path. "No, really, that's okay," Greta said, half running to keep up with his fast strides. "If you could just lay it across the roof of my car . . ."

But either he wasn't listening or he was intentionally ignoring her. He headed straight for his truck and set the mattress down in the large bed, then grabbed the box from the passenger seat of her Bug.

Great. Even though she was undeniably grateful for his help, she sure hated playing damsel in distress.

* * *

Seated in the passenger side of Gray's Ford for the short ride to her new place, Greta realized she was in an awkward position. Because Gray had helped her, she now felt obligated to be nice to him, the fiancé of the woman who had destroyed her life.

As Gray turned left off her old street, she cleared her throat and glanced over at him. Warm air came rushing through the open window, ruffling his hair. "So, if you don't mind my asking, why did you become a lawyer in the first place? If you don't like conflict and all."

Gray shrugged as he slowed for a stop sign. "My dad. It was his big dream for me. He worked as a ski-lift operator for a lot of years before he married my mom. Her father owned half of Aspen back then. Before that, I guess my dad was pretty poor. Happy enough, though. He lived to ski, and he got to do a lot of it. Still, he'd also always dreamed of being a lawyer someday. And even though he got pretty involved in Aspen real estate once he and my mom got married, he never made it to law school."

"So you went for him."

He flashed her an ironic grin. "Yep. But after he started getting sick, he told me he felt bad for pushing me to law school, that I should do what I wanted."

Greta nodded. "Architecture."

"Uh-huh."

"Turn right up here."

As Gray switched on his turn signal, he again smiled over at her. "I wanted to design things, see them emerge from nothing to slowly become my vision. This is going to be my first big job."

"Nice perk," Greta said without thinking and winced

at the bitter edge in it. *Play nice*, she scolded herself. He glanced over at her, his dark brows furrowed in a question. "Of being with Stephanie Harwood, I meant." The words now lacked the punch she'd originally intended.

She pointed to her new apartment building, and Gray pulled up alongside the curb. After turning the ignition off, he turned to face her, his mouth a tight line of either anger or frustration. "I'm with Stephanie because I love her."

"Well, bully for you," Greta muttered, as once again she spoke first, thought after.

Gray shook his head, definitely frustrated now. "Look, she's not a bad person. Like I told you before, she's just trying to prove herself to her father, prove she can be as successful as her brother, if given half a chance."

"Enter Winter's Haven," Greta said, her jaw tight.

Gray shrugged and let out a breath. "It's her baby."

Greta bit her lip to stop herself from saying anything else she might regret. Without another word, she opened the door and climbed out of the truck.

Chapter Fifteen

Gray's throat constricted at the sight of Greta's new apartment building, a dated adobe-style place with cheap stucco that had chipped off in large chunks, showing the gray concrete blocks beneath. Hopefully it would be very temporary.

He hauled the mattress out of the truck bed and carried it up to the door of her apartment, as Greta grabbed the box. When Greta opened the front door, Gray's eyes widened at the sight of the crowded living room.

"I know," Greta said, puffing away a loose curl from her lips. "I'm moving a lot of this stuff to storage later."

"Need some help?" He'd asked the question automatically but then thought twice about it. After their . . . moment in her shop two weeks earlier, he'd vowed to stay away from Greta Kendall. That day, looking down at her lovely, troubled face, he'd felt something emerging in him, something warm and tender and sweet that needed to be immediately squelched.

And he'd tried. The minute she'd emerged from her house the next morning, he'd quickly climbed into his truck, intending to drive away fast. But she'd stopped him, mistakenly thinking he'd slipped that envelope into her mailbox, and lured him into her house with the promise of pancakes. He should have said no, but he really *did* love a good pancake, and Stephanie never made them, forever mindful of the pudgy preteen she'd been. Maybe he should have learned how himself.

But apart from that wonderful pancake breakfast, he *had* stayed away from Greta, even though he really did need to start on the final design. He'd delayed going back on-site until she'd moved out—which was supposed to be yesterday. And yet there she'd been this morning. But something inside him had been undeniably happy to see her. And she looked so dang cute in her shorts and T-shirt, her curls piled on top of her head in a wonderfully messy ponytail. Oh yes, she was trouble, wasn't she? So why the offer to help?

Guilt, came the immediate answer. It killed him to see her move out of her beautiful house and into this small, sad place.

Thankfully, Greta shook her head. "No thanks. I've got some help coming."

Gray nodded and hoisted up the mattress. He began steering it through the room, but needed Greta's help in navigating through the boxes and assorted pieces of furniture. They finally made it to the back bedroom where Adele would be staying and set the mattress down just outside the door.

Gray glanced in the room and let out a low whistle. "Wow." Greta followed his eyes to the headboard, an intricate design of leaves and branches carved in a large block of wood.

She nodded, pride sparkling in her big brown eyes. "My grandfather did that."

Gray leaned in to get a better look at it. The wood was darker at the edges, as if it had been charred. "It looks like . . . Is it a door?"

Again, Greta nodded. "It's from my grandparents' first house out by the edge of town. It got struck by lightning and burned to the ground. All that was left was the chimney and the front door. It must have been blown out and away early on in the fire. My grandfather carved it into a headboard, wanting to bring just one piece of their old house along with them."

"It's amazing. Your grandfather was a real artist."

Greta looked up fondly at the headboard, her eyes roaming across it as if seeing it for the first time. "He was, wasn't he?" Then she sighed and looked up at the mattress. "All right, let's finish up with this bad boy."

Gray nodded and together they lifted up the mattress, wrangling it around a chest of drawers, a chair, and finally the corner of the bed frame.

As they were lining it up next to the frame in the tight space between the wall and the bed, Gray's foot came down on something soft and squishy. Automatically he jerked away from it, his reflexes honed from accidentally stepping on Stephanie's cat, Sprinkles. His ankles still bore the many jagged scars of those encounters.

He lost his balance and instinctively yanked back on the mattress to keep himself from falling, but that made the mattress lean perilously overhead, threatening to squash them both against the wall.

He overcompensated, pushing too hard the other way, and the mattress tipped over fast and began plunging down toward the bed frame. The wall behind them blocked their getting away, and as the mattress fell, the bottom of it swept them both up and they dropped with it.

Greta let out a little scream that ended with a hiccup of laughter, as she thudded down on the mattress and tumbled down right on top of Gray.

Warm. She was so warm, the skin of her bare legs and arms soft and sleek grazing against his own skin.

"Oh!" Startled, she pulled away from him, extricating her arms and legs. "Sorry."

"No problem." Gray heard the husky undertone in his voice.

Greta let out a little chuckle, although it sounded a bit forced. "Well, you definitely didn't miss your calling as a mover, did you? You're not very good at it."

Gray lifted his hands defensively. "Hey, it wasn't my fault. I think I stepped on your cat."

Her brows creased. "My what?"

"Your . . ." With a curious frown he reached over the side of the mattress and picked up a throw pillow.

Greta burst out a laugh. "Hey, it's Fluffy! Come here, sweetie pie. I've missed you." She grabbed the pillow from him and began stroking its "fur."

Gray rolled his eyes, trying to be annoyed at her for making fun of him, but he ended up laughing himself. He eyed the pillow critically. "You know, your cat's looking a little . . . square. Is that a problem?"

"Ha-ha," she said perfunctorily. Her smile fading, Greta plucked at a few loose threads in the corner of the pillow. "Anyway, thanks for your help. I really appreciate it." Her gaze flickered up to meet his.

"You're welcome."

A blush appeared high on her cheekbones, and she looked back down at the pillow.

"You know," he said after a moment, keeping his voice soft, almost a whisper, "I wish I *had* left that photo in your mailbox."

She glanced up at him again, and this time didn't look away. Neither did he. The feeling he'd had in her shop two weeks earlier returned, but stronger now, as if it had continued to grow on its own all this time. Watching the muscles of her face soften, he suspected he wasn't alone in that.

As the first wisps of desire began swirling in her eyes, Gray realized he could no longer fight it. He reached for her, cupping her cheek gently in his hand. She didn't move.

With his thumb, Gray slowly traced the line of her mouth. He closed his eyes, and for just a moment allowed himself to think about what it would be like to kiss those silken lips of hers.

But then he pulled his hand away, his eyes blinking open. He didn't know what was going on with him, with all this. But one thing he *did* know was that he was no cheater. And in his book, kissing another woman was most definitely cheating, perhaps the worst kind because of its intimacy. Even *thinking* about it was dangerous.

"I'm sorry, Greta. I shouldn't have done that."

He saw the emotion sweep through her eyes, a complex blend of helplessness, humiliation, and yes, lingering desire.

"Oh, hello, Gray, nice to see you again." It was Adele, standing at the door.

Greta's mouth, so tender and soft under his touch a

moment earlier, hardened into a tight, unyielding line. "Oh, you don't have to be nice to him, Mom." Gray was taken aback by the sudden venom in Greta's voice.

Adele's eyes widened. "Whyever not?"

"Oh, *lots* of reasons." Greta shot Gray a nasty, condemning look. "Mostly because he's the reason we lost the house. Together with his *fiancée*."

Adele's face crumpled in confusion and disappointment as she turned to Gray. "You? But why? Why would you do that to us?"

Gray winced. It was like getting slapped in the face. "I'm sorry," he said to Adele and then turned to Greta. "I'm sorry," he said again, no longer apologizing for the house. Still, it rang hollow with inadequacy.

"Hello? Anyone home?" Gray recognized the voice. Jack Fenton. "Sorry I'm late. My deposition ran—" As he appeared at the door, Fenton stopped, clearly surprised to see Gray. He raised his eyebrows at Greta.

"Mr. Daniels was just leaving." Greta stood up and stared at Gray, flat and expectant.

"Yes," Gray muttered, "I was."

He got to his feet and beelined it out of there, unable to look any one of them in the eye.

"He seemed like such a nice young man," he heard Adele say from behind him and felt a fresh avalanche of shame tumble down on him. Oh, the disappointment in her eyes.

As he walked through the crowded living room, Gray slammed his shin against the coffee table, and he sucked in air, holding back several choice expletives. But not just about his shin and the welt already forming there. And not over his guilt at how badly he'd wanted to kiss Greta Kendall, either.

No, jealousy seared hot and sharp through him now. Undeniable. Still, it was different from when Stephanie used to tease him in high school and then college, mentioning other guys in her study groups or numerous clubs who asked her out. He'd just get angry back then. But it was a surface kind of anger.

This he felt in the pit of his stomach, the core of him. And he had no right to it. Absolutely no right.

"He was helping me move some stuff over from the other house," Greta said, responding to the unspoken question in Jack's eyes.

Clearly, it hadn't satisfied him. "What? But why? You knew I was coming. And why *him*? I mean, did you forget who he is?"

Oh, yes, she had forgotten, hadn't she? Especially in that moment when Gray was cupping her cheek, running his thumb across her mouth. Blood still pulsed strong there in slow, warm beats.

"I know exactly who he is," Greta grumbled. It sounded harsh and defensive in her ears. She looked down, suddenly unable to meet Jack's eyes, the accusation lingering in them. She had no defense against it.

Heck, she'd *wanted* Gray to kiss her, had in fact done nothing to stop it. *He'd* been the one to stop it. An engaged man—what did that make her? Greta let out a long breath as the shame and humiliation began to really set in.

She noticed a bright orange piece of paper crumpled in

Jack's hand. "This was on your door," he mumbled and handed it to her. Greta had to smooth it out to read it.

SAVE THE GINGERBREAD HOUSE!
TOMORROW, 3 P.M. AT TOWN HALL.
LET YOUR VOICE BE HEARD!

Penny's work.

Greta let out a breath. It seemed so pointless. She just wanted to move on now. Accept reality and try to work through the misery of wanting the impossible.

She let out a dry chuckle as she followed Jack back out to the living room.

Was she still talking about the house?

Chapter Sixteen

The next morning Greta headed outside to the bank of mailboxes by the street. She stuck her key in the slot, opened the box, and immediately spotted the manila envelope crammed inside.

Her heart leaped in her chest. Another potential reprieve from her mysterious benefactor?

She yanked out the envelope, slid her finger under the flap at one end, and ripped it open. Holding her breath, she pulled out the piece of paper inside. The breath came out as a groan.

It wasn't a reprieve at all, but a photograph of her and her ex, Mark, taken at the Cherished Memories Chapel in Las Vegas on their wedding day. The number 11 was scrawled in one corner and jaggedly circled in red marker.

Greta shook her head, angry at herself as she slammed the little door shut. If she'd taken the time to turn the blasted envelope over, she would've seen the address written on it, the familiar block letters partially covered by the bright yellow sticker with her forwarding address on it.

Unable to stop herself, she turned the photo over to read the note she knew she'd find there. "I *will* have you again," the "will" underlined three times.

Greta shuddered. She knew he meant it in every sense

of the word. To possess her, mind, body, and spirit. And he had, hadn't he? Gradually, insidiously, Mark had isolated her from her family and her friends over the course of just a few months. Whenever someone would call for her, he'd frown and act put out. Even Penny.

The first couple of semesters after Greta moved to Denver and Penny had stayed in Spector to work at her parents' bakery, the two of them used to gab away happily for hours at a time at least twice a week, talking about everything and nothing. But under Mark's glare, Greta found herself truncating everything she said and cutting the conversations short. She could hear the hurt in Penny's voice but felt powerless to change it.

After a couple of months, the calls had sputtered to every couple of weeks, and then once a month, if even that. Penny's hurt had turned into anger, and she'd finally told Greta she wouldn't be calling anymore. Thankfully, Penny had forgiven her once she'd learned the truth about Mark.

Greta heaved out a sigh, leaned against the bank of mailboxes, and looked at the photo again. It had all seemed so romantic, the spur of the moment decision to elope, the trip to Las Vegas. Now it just seemed sad.

In the photo, she was wearing the cheap dress she'd gotten at a thrift store a couple of blocks off the strip: Brides-R-Us. Boy, had *that* been a depressing moment. All her life surrounded by the most beautiful wedding dresses ever made, hours spent dreaming of what hers would look like, ivory or white, satin or taffeta. And there she was picking out a secondhand one, buying someone else's choices.

But money had been tight, and it was the best they could do. They'd gotten even more of a discount on the dress because of a purple stain on the left side of the bodice. But as the clerk pointed out, if Greta held her bouquet just a shade lower than felt natural, the stain would be covered completely.

Mark had called around and found a cheap chapel, which just so happened to have a drive-thru option. Greta had always thought that was a joke, but no, they were the real deal. Mark thought it would be a hoot.

The Cherished Memories Chapel was far down on the strip, an obvious conversion from a fast-food joint, tacos probably, judging from the carved archways of the doors and windows. A roof had been built over the drive-thru lane with a mural painted on the ceiling, faded letters spelling out THE PASSAGE OF LOVE.

They'd opted for the cheapest package available. A hundred and twenty-nine bucks had gotten them a bottle of nearly flat champagne, twelve eight-by-ten photos, music, a silk bouquet she didn't get to keep, use of the chapel's beat-up limousine for the duration of the ceremony, and last but not least, matching bride and groom T-shirts.

Mark had thrown a fit at the end when they'd asked for forty bucks more, a donation for the minister. He'd tossed out a twenty and said they were lucky to get that. The minister's wife had flashed a wry smile at Greta. "Good luck, honey. You'll need it with that one."

Nice start to a life of wedded bliss.

As indicated in the corner, this was photo number 11 out of the 12. Mark had sent them periodically over the years, each with a note similar to this one scrawled on the back.

Greta brought the photo up closer and really looked at

herself, her face, her eyes. There was happiness there, to be sure, but something dark lingered in them too, didn't it? As if she'd known even on that day that trouble was looming on the horizon.

Never in a million years did she think she'd find herself in that situation. Although she hadn't consciously been aware of it, she realized now she had always looked down a little on battered wives or girlfriends, seeing them as weak. No way would she let anything like that happen to her.

She let out a harsh, bitter chuckle. It had just been so slow and gradual, like watching a plant grow. You never actually saw it happen, but then one day you woke up in the emergency room and there it was.

Shaking her head, Greta headed back toward the apartment. She'd been such a different person back then. But a moment later she frowned, pausing at the door. Had she? Had she really been so different? And more to the point, could it happen again? Not with Mark obviously, but maybe with someone else.

Would she see it coming this time? Or would she be blinded by love again, all else falling away as he caught her eye from across the room and smiled that slow, sweet smile of his, those almond-shaped green eyes taking on that sexy gleam that always set a thousand tingles loose in her belly?

No, she wouldn't let it happen again. Even if she had to be alone the rest of her life. Jaw set, she marched inside, went straight into the kitchen, and grabbed the trash can from under the sink, slamming the cabinet door closed.

Sitting down at the table, she began ripping up the photo

in angry little shreds that rained down into the trash can. The pieces of paper blurred as tears sprang in her eyes.

"Greta?" her mother called from her workroom. "Is everything all right?"

Greta swallowed hard. "Yes, Mom, everything's fine."

Chapter Seventeen

A little after five that afternoon, a knock came at the door of the apartment.

"I'll get it, Mom!" Greta laid the flower-girl dress she was working on down on the sofa beside her. As per her six-year-old client's request, she was adding one more ruffle along the bottom.

Grateful to be able to move more freely around the room now that the boxes were gone, Greta walked over to the door and opened it. Deputy Sheriff Liam Shaw stood there in full uniform. Liam was Patrick Shaw's younger brother, two years behind them during their school years.

"Hi, Liam, how are you?"

"Good, good," he said with that timid smile of his. He had a shy sweetness about him that ran completely counter to his job. "Look, Greta, we have some trouble brewing down at town hall. I thought you should know."

Greta frowned. "What kind of trouble?"

"Well, you know Penny's protest rally was today."

Greta drew in a sharp breath. She'd forgotten all about it. "Did something happen?"

"No, but Penny's about to be arrested. She's in the council chambers refusing to leave and they're fixing to close up for the night. I was hoping you could—"

"Let's go," Greta cut in, and then called inside the apartment, "Mom! I'm going out for a little while!"

Greta burst into the council chambers followed by Liam. And there she was, her enormously pregnant friend, seated on the floor next to the door. Her very own sit-in.

The hard determination that had been on Penny's dear face softened into hurt when she saw Greta. "Where were you? I thought you'd come."

Greta knelt down on her knees in front of Penny and took both her hands in hers. "Oh, Penny, I'm so sorry. I got another wedding picture from Mark today and I guess I got distracted."

Penny's face, a little puffy from her pregnancy, scrunched up in sudden hatred. "That creep."

Greta nodded. "Yeah. And I let him get under my skin again, making me . . . well, you know. Otherwise, you know I would've been here."

"I know."

"But, Penny, what are you doing? You're about to be arrested!"

Fierce determination again gleamed in Penny's eyes as she glanced over at Liam. "I know. I want to be."

Greta shook her head adamantly. "But Pen, your getting arrested is not going to do any good. It's over. We've done everything we could, fought as hard as we could." She gave her a sad pragmatic shrug. "We lost."

Tears glimmered in Penny's eyes. "I know. I just wanted to make a statement."

Greta gave her friend a fond smile and felt tears welling in her own eyes. "You have made a statement. And I love you too."

At that, Penny burst into a sob. "But your house . . ."

"We'll be fine." Greta shrugged again, aiming for casual. "It was too big for just the two of us anyway. Change will do us good. Isn't that what they say?" Greta had tried to instill some confidence in her voice and thought maybe she'd succeeded when she saw Penny nodding. "Besides, you don't want your baby born in jail do you?"

Penny laughed through her tears. "No." Her face suddenly brightened. "Ooh, I know! A boycott! That'll make a statement for sure. Here, help me up, will you? I've got a lot of work to do."

Greta signaled Liam over to help her and together they hoisted Penny up.

As they emerged from the front door of the town hall, a cheer went up from the dozen or so people that had remained from Penny's rally. Ian and Gregor Koslovsky were both busy snapping pictures.

Penny waddled up and stood in front of the little crowd, her face again radiating determination. "Listen up, everyone! We're going to organize a countywide boycott of Winter's Haven!" The crowd cheered again.

Penny cupped her hands around her mouth and began chanting, "Boycott the mall! Boycott the mall!"

As the crowd took up the chant, Greta grinned. Her friend was officially out of the gate. Nothing would stop her now.

*   *   *

Gray pulled up in front of the house next door to Greta's. He let out a dark chuckle as he shut off the motor. *The house next door to Greta's?* As opposed to simply 130 Lamont Street. So now he was relating everything to her?

"Focus," he mumbled to himself. "You have a job to do here."

He shoved away all thoughts of her, something he'd been doing a lot lately. He'd learned to replace them with thoughts of Stephanie through the years, memories he'd always held close to his heart. Skiing with her as kids, summer picnics, camping together, their first kiss when they were eight.

They'd been ice skating on the small pond behind her house that froze over every winter. Without warning, she'd suddenly sped toward him, lost control, and grabbed on to him, pulling him down with her.

Gray had fallen nearly on top of her and, for a moment, he'd just looked down at her. Gosh, she'd looked so beautiful, her face glowing with excitement and cold, her blue eyes intent on his. He remembered wondering if she'd done it deliberately, anticipating a kiss.

Even now, he could remember vividly the feel of her lips against his, plump and soft, a little chilled just on the surface. It had been a truly perfect moment.

Unexpectedly, Greta Kendall jumped right back into his mind then, and the memory of her flushed face when they'd fallen on top of the mattress, her curls partially covering her face.

"Would you stop?" he scolded himself, angrily grabbing his clipboard from the seat beside him.

Climbing out of the truck, he deliberately averted his eyes from Greta's house and walked up to 130 Lamont.

For a moment he stared up at the old Queen Anne, appreciating the clean strong angles of her lines, the soft curves of the turret and porch roof. A frown tugged at the corners of his mouth. What a waste.

He hadn't known, when he'd first broached the idea of designing Winter's Haven with Stephanie, that people—namely Greta Kendall and her mother—were being forced out of their homes. As he'd told Greta, he'd become an architect to design things, to build them, not to tear them down.

Gray heaved out a breath. He almost wished they were already gone, these old houses. It was so hard to see his vision for the mall when they were still here. They were like . . . dead houses, their spirits already gone, now only awaiting the final act, like condemned inmates in prison.

He and Stephanie had come up to Spector the morning they tore down the house next to Greta's. Stephanie had wanted to watch. Gray had tried hard to ignore the uncomfortable feeling that prickled through him when she'd said that.

He hadn't really wanted to come himself, but a small piece of him had wanted to see Greta, see how she was holding up. Or so he tried to convince himself.

After the first couple of minutes of destruction he hadn't been able to watch anymore, struck by the sheer brutality of it all, and had shifted his gaze to Greta's house. And there she'd been, standing in a side window on the second floor. Her bedroom perhaps?

Her eyes had been riveted on the scene below her. As Gray watched, her chin had begun quivering, her eyes gleaming with tears.

He'd silently urged her to look over at him, to see him. He thought he could somehow relay some measure of comfort to her so she'd know that someone else there cared. But she hadn't seen him, her eyes glued to the house next door.

Adele had appeared at the other window then, and she too had begun crying. Watching Greta pull her away, Gray had felt his breakfast stir uncomfortably in his stomach.

His eyes flickered involuntary to Greta's house now, and he stopped short. The front door was wide open! Vandals, he immediately thought. He supposed at this point it didn't really matter what was done to the house. Still, it seemed somehow indecent, a violation. Like kicking a man when he was down.

He hurried up the front steps and walked inside.

Chapter Eighteen

How she yearned for this, ached for it. Greta leaned forward a few inches, just enough to close the distance between them. She shut her eyes, her heart racing in anticipation.

Somewhere inside her she knew she was only dreaming, but she'd wanted it so badly that day she allowed it to continue now.

And then she felt Gray's lips, soft and impossibly smooth, just barely brush across her own. She'd wanted the kiss to deepen but before it could, she awoke breathless, her lips tingling and warm. She touched her fingertips to her mouth and savored the fleeting memory there, now only the ghost of a kiss. She knew it was all she would ever get.

Greta yawned and sat up on the couch. Wincing, she stretched out the sore muscles of her back. The night before, she'd spent hours taking in an especially intricate Christian Lacroix dress with ruffles gathered along one side. The bride needed to pick it up this morning, so Greta stayed up late finishing it.

She glanced at her watch: three thirty. She'd napped for nearly two hours! But clearly, she had needed the rest.

For the last two weeks since the move, she and her

mother had been working feverishly on dozens of dresses for anxious brides. She hadn't taken any new orders since the day of her final defeat, but they still had a lot to finish up.

Greta let out a long breath, her shoulders sagging. This used to be such a wonderful time of year for her and her mother—"happy busy," they'd always called it. But that was back in the old house, when they'd had enough space to work in. This place was much too small. Yards and yards of taffeta, lace, tulle, and satin filled her mother's workroom, overflowing into the living room.

Soon only the Mainbocher would remain. It had taken a backseat for a few days while Greta searched for matching beads. After spending hours e-mailing close-ups of them to dozens of stores, she'd finally found a perfect match in a small bead shop in New York City. They'd arrived only yesterday.

Across from her on the coffee table, Greta's phone vibrated in her purse. She lunged for it, trying to get to it before the ultraloud ringtone she'd selected kicked in. She'd wanted it loud, not wanting to miss any calls these days. Her brides didn't like it when they couldn't get in touch with her. And she had more than a few 'zillas who demanded constant updates.

Greta took a peek at the caller ID before answering. Gray Daniels. She paused, her thumb hovering above the answer button. Her other hand was halfway up, about to smooth the bedhead out of her curls when she realized what she was doing. *He's on the phone, dummy. And you're mad at him, remember? Oh yeah, and he's engaged.*

Shaking her head at her own daftness, Greta pressed

the button. "Hello?" It came out a bit squeaky, still rough from sleep.

"Your mother's here. At your house."

"What?" Greta jumped up from the couch and ran over to her mother's workroom. She was gone.

"I saw the front door was open," Gray was saying. "I checked inside and found her."

"Is she okay?" Greta demanded as she grabbed her keys and purse.

"She's fine. She's sitting on the stairs here just staring out at nothing. She's pretty unresponsive, but seems okay otherwise."

"I'll be right there."

"Mom?" Greta called inside as she pushed the door open and walked in.

There she was, just as Gray had said, sitting on the stairs, staring off into space. Gray sat a couple of steps behind her.

As she headed over to them, Greta's heels echoed through the empty house, emphasizing the newfound loneliness of the place.

She leaned in front of her mother, taking in the vacant expression in Adele's brown eyes. "I was taking a nap," she said, feeling suddenly compelled to explain. "I didn't realize she was gone."

Gray reached forward to hand her a key. "It was in the door."

Greta stood up and took it, shaking her head. "I didn't even think to take it away from her." She let out a stark chuckle. "I mean, in a couple of weeks the locks aren't even going to exist anymore, are they?"

She sat down beside Adele and wrapped her arms around her. Her mother stiffened under the embrace, which made a lump form in Greta's throat. She released her, and her mother seemed to relax, although her eyes were still void of any true emotion. Greta glanced up at Gray. "I hate it when she does this, wandering away. It scares me."

Gray nodded sympathetically. "My dad only did it a couple of times. I guess he took most of his walks only in his mind."

Greta nodded and at that moment remembered she was supposed to be mad at him.

Oh, forget it. She didn't have the energy.

"Come on, Mom, let's get you home." Greta put her arm around her mother's waist and pulled up gently.

Adele suddenly gripped her arm, her eyes wide and pleading, radiating pure desperation.

"My daughter, that man's hurt her. They just called from the hospital. I have to get to Denver. Do you know where my keys are?"

"I'm fine, Mom. I'm right here."

Tears brimmed in Adele's eyes and spilled over. "Please, my keys. I need to . . ."

Her voice trailed off as her eyes emptied of emotion, becoming vacant once again. Bittersweet relief washed through Greta.

"All right, let's go, Mom." Her mother walked beside her automatically, her face blank. Greta let out a breath. She didn't know which was worse, this haunting blankness or the sheer panic of a few minutes earlier.

"Don't bother closing it," she said, as Gray followed them

outside. But from behind her, she heard the click of the door.

"It wouldn't seem right," Gray muttered.

None of this is right, Greta thought.

As they headed down the path for the last time, Greta glanced over to the left and saw that the house there, home to a charming pottery shop only a couple of months ago, was gone now too. Vanished. Even the basement walls had been removed, a century-old house reduced to a massive dirt hole.

At the sight of it, and knowing hers was close behind, Greta felt a sob rising. She swallowed hard to keep it at bay.

For once, Greta was grateful her mother wasn't aware and so hadn't noticed the absence of their other neighbor's house. She did come around a little, though, as Greta was helping her into the car. "Greta?" she said, blinking.

Greta sighed at the now familiar confusion in her mother's voice. "You're fine, Mom," she said, clicking in the strap of her mother's seat belt. "We're going home."

Her mother frowned, looking up at the house. "But we are home."

Greta let out another breath. "Not anymore."

As she closed the door, Greta saw the lost and bewildered look in her mother's eyes and again swallowed hard. But she was too late this time, and she choked on a sudden sob. She closed the door and leaned against the car for a moment, tears spilling over onto her cheeks. She wiped them away but felt more brimming.

Gray had taken a step closer when he saw she was crying, and Greta looked up at him, shaking her head miserably. "I remember how she used to be, you know? I want my old mom back." Her voice broke on the last word.

Out of the corner of her eyes, Greta saw Gray raise his hand toward her face, and she instantly flinched back, hard and fast.

Surprised, Gray stopped and retreated a step, his brows creasing. "I was just— There was a curl there. Stuck." He motioned toward her face, and then Greta felt the strand of hair snared in the wetness of her cheek. "I didn't mean to—"

"No, it's okay." Greta brushed the hair away and gave Gray a meek smile. "Sorry about that. My ex."

"Oh." He nodded, the blue in his eyes darkening. "Were you together a long time?"

"A year. I met him at Colorado State, and we eloped after one semester together. It really hurt my parents, but he insisted. And I was so in love with him. But afterward, he dropped the nice-guy act, and the ugliness came through loud and clear."

Greta shook her head. "I should have left the first time he raised his hand in that threatening way of his. I kept thinking it was a onetime thing, but then it was like a ten-time thing, and then one day I got gel deodorant instead of solid and—" She blinked and felt her face warm. "Gosh, why am I telling you all this?"

Gray raised one shoulder in a sympathetic shrug. "Because you need to talk about it, and you don't want to burden your mother."

Greta nodded slowly, considering that. As she did, she realized she was rubbing her right wrist where . . . She yanked her hand away with a shudder. She didn't want to go back there. "Anyway, he's in jail now, so I don't have to worry about him anymore."

Pulling her keys out of her pocket, she looked up at the house and let out a rush of air. "So when's my house's date with the wrecking ball?"

"A week from today." Gray's voice was low, rough. He took a step closer, not smiling. "Look, I really wish there was something I could do . . ."

But Greta gave him a resigned shrug. "There's nothing *to* do, is there? It's a done deal. No more appeals." With a wry smile, she looked down at her mother, staring off vacantly again through the car window. "My mom's not going to get her fairy-tale ending this time."

"Please, Greta." Gray touched her arm, his eyes imploring and helpless.

She looked down at his hand and then found herself smiling sadly up at him. "And you're certainly not my knight in shining armor."

She pulled her arm gently away and headed around the car to the driver's side. "Good-bye, Gray," she said over the roof.

Just before she turned away, she thought she saw his strong chin tremble, tears glistening in his dark eyes.

Standing alone at the curb, Gray swiped at his eyes as he watched Greta drive away with her mother.

Guilt crashed over him in wave after unrelenting wave. He hated having been a part of her misery. And she'd already had such a hard time. What had her ex-husband done to her to end up in jail?

Gray shook his head as he let out a mirthless chuckle. He was supposed to be so happy right now, with the wedding less than two weeks away. If only—

And that was when he got the idea.

After he'd told Stephanie what he wanted to do, all she did was shrug.

"And I'll use some of the money my mom left me so you won't lose your cost-efficiency rating with your father." The last part sounded harsh to Gray's ears, but Stephanie didn't seem to notice. She only shrugged again.

"It's your money." She cocked her head to one side then, focusing her gaze on him, studious and assessing. "Why do you care so much, anyway?" Was that jealousy glinting in those cornflower blue eyes of hers? If so, he'd be surprised. He'd always played that role in their relationship, never her. She probably wouldn't even view Greta Kendall as a threat. Her mistake.

Stephanie's smile, curious but distant, bothered Gray. "Why don't *you*? I mean, you're messing with people's lives here."

"I know that, Gray." Stephanie let out a long sigh, as once again her features relaxed out of hard-nosed mode. She met his eyes and held them. "I understand people are getting hurt. I get that. I mean, I'm no monster. But at the same time, don't you think you're being a little naïve? With progress comes sacrifice. It's always been that way."

Gray let out a bitter grunt. "Right. Eminent domain."

"Well, yes, that's the ugly truth of it, isn't it? And of course it's sad that some people get trampled on—of course I feel bad about that. But it's reality." She lifted her shoulders in a thoughtful shrug. "I guess I've learned to compartmentalize it, the painful parts of it. I have to."

Gray said nothing, only let out a long, slow breath. He wasn't going to get anywhere with this.

She flashed him a fond smile. "You know, it's a good thing you're quitting law. You'd go broke taking care of all the sad sacks."

Gray nodded, not smiling. "Probably."

At that, Stephanie crossed her arms and Gray sighed, seeing the ruthless developer in her once again take over. "You know what I think? I think you're too sweet for your own good."

Then she lifted a hand to his face and patted the side of his cheek. He hated when she did that. It made him feel like he was five years old.

Chapter Nineteen

Greta raised the unfamiliar wand to her eyelashes and stroked on a little more mascara. Of course it got all clumped up in one corner. She was a bit of an alien in the mysterious world of makeup. But you were supposed to get yourself all snazzed up when you went on a date, right? It had been a long time, but she thought she at least remembered that rule.

She dabbed a tissue against the clump, but succeeded only in smushing a glop into the corner of her eye. "Ow!"

Automatically she pressed her palm against the stinging and felt the wet mascara smear all around her eye. *Great.* She let out a breath. Gray Daniels was to blame for this.

Since her divorce, she'd ignored this part of life— dating, romance. Sealed it off. But as much as she hated to admit it, Gray had cracked open that seal just a little, made her catch a glimpse of what she'd been missing for so long.

And so when Jack asked her out to dinner tonight, making it clear it was a date and not business, she thought maybe she'd try cracking open that seal a bit further herself. It would be a good distraction too. Her house was slated for demolition in only a few short days.

She just wished she was more excited about tonight. So

far she just didn't feel any sparks with Jack. But maybe that was a good thing. She'd had sparks galore with Mark, and look where she'd ended up.

Besides, maybe new sparks would take a while. She needed to at least give them a chance. With fresh resolve, Greta went into the bathroom and began washing her face.

Clean slate.

Gray pulled into a spot in the visitor's lot across the street from Greta's apartment and switched off the engine. He glanced toward her door, aware that his heart was beating a hair faster than it should have been. He wanted to tell her in person, though. After spending the day figuring out how it was all going to work, he now knew for sure.

His hand was pressing down on the latch when her door opened. And there she was, wearing the flowing lavender dress she'd worn that first day in her shop. She'd done something different with her hair, braided the sides loosely back. Gray smiled. She looked like a medieval queen standing there.

But then Fenton appeared behind her, and Gray felt his smile slip. As they walked down the path toward the street, Gray got a better look at her face and saw she was wearing lipstick. He couldn't remember her ever wearing makeup before.

She was smiling up at Fenton, but there was a polite edge to it, not one of the more natural smiles she'd flashed so many times during their pancake breakfast, back when she'd thought he was an ally.

Gray thought a lot about that morning. He'd been so

comfortable there, so completely himself. Ever since then, even though he'd made a conscious effort *not* to think about it, his thoughts would drift back there, and he'd find himself smiling as he remembered something Greta or Adele had said.

Fenton's hand grazed across Greta's lower back as they headed toward an ancient Bronco and jealousy again burned through Gray, quickly followed by an intense guilt he could not talk himself out of.

All right, so he *was* attracted to Greta. No choice but to admit that now.

And that was exactly why he couldn't talk to her again. Not in person. He'd just leave her a voice mail and be done with it. The feelings would fade. His love for Stephanie went back so many years, decades, and this—whatever it was—had only been around a few weeks.

The feelings couldn't run that deep.

Chapter Twenty

Aren't you going to get that?" her mother asked through a mouthful of pins. Greta's cell was ringing in the other room.

"Nope." Across from her mother, Greta snipped some thread off the seam of the Mainbocher.

She should probably just turn off the ringer of her phone. Now that brides were no longer calling her, Greta had taken to not answering her phone the last couple of days, unable to bear the sympathy half the town wanted to convey about the impending demolition of her house. She'd sat through several of those painful calls and decided she didn't need to do that anymore.

And so she'd begun letting everything go through to voice mail. When she was ready she'd listen to the voice mails, return the calls, and thank everyone for their support. Just not right now.

The phone stopped ringing in the other room. Finally. Greta felt her mother's eyes on her, could sense the waves of disapproval flowing toward her. Okay, yes, she was being rude. But she was entitled to a little alone time to wallow, wasn't she?

The phone rang again, and her mother scowled over

at Greta and then stood, walked into the other room, and answered it.

Fantastic. Here we go again.

"Hello? Well, hi there! How are you? Just a sec, I'll get her." Her mother came back in, holding the phone out to Greta. "It's Jack."

With a sigh Greta took the phone. Jack was such a good man, handsome, kind, and caring. And she'd definitely had a good time with him during their dinner. He was so smart, and quick with little jokes and insightful comments.

At the end of the night when he was dropping her off, she'd caught his gaze wandering down to her mouth, but kissing him hadn't felt right to her. Maybe she needed those blasted sparks to make it feel right. And so she'd given him a quick hug instead.

"It's okay," he'd murmured in her ear. "Whenever you're ready." Still, a hurt-puppy expression had found its way into his eyes, something Greta didn't find attractive at all. That was why she was surprised to feel herself smiling into the phone as she greeted him.

Not quite a spark yet, but definitely something.

Chapter Twenty-one

On "Demolition Tuesday," or so she'd dubbed it, Greta wanted to be as far away from Spector, Colorado, as possible. And so she and her mother drove down to Denver for a couple of days.

They saw *Cats* at the Buell Theater in the performing-arts complex downtown and the next day took in a new Monet exhibit at the Denver Art Museum. They stayed at the Brown Palace Hotel, where her mother and father had spent their wedding night.

For most of the trip, Adele remained lucid, something Greta cherished more and more each day. On the return trip, though, an hour outside of Aspen, Adele had grown silent and unresponsive, becoming lost in her mind somewhere. And judging from the taut, upset look in her eyes, it wasn't a happy place. Greta hoped her own dismal mood hadn't affected her mother. She'd tried to act upbeat during the trip, but she was no actress.

They returned to Spector just before eight that night. After a late supper, Greta put her mother to bed and then got back in her car and forced herself to drive by the house—or lack thereof.

Part of her still didn't really believe it. She thought

seeing it gone would finally make it real. Then she could feel the grief, work through it, and move on, get to a better place in her head.

Driving up her old street, Greta kept her head averted even as she parked in front. She turned off the ignition, drew in a breath and turned to face reality.

The breath came gushing out from her lungs, tears instantly filling her eyes.

It was gone. It was really gone. Only the brick path remained, heading nowhere now, the phlox on either side of it trampled flat.

A pretty pink petal landed on the side window and, for a moment, Greta just stared at it. Seeing it so close, so real . . . And then she was crying.

For a while Greta just sat there and let the tears come, not even bothering to wipe them away. She just felt so utterly and completely bereft.

And she suspected it was more than just the house making her feel that way.

Chapter Twenty-two

What idiots. Smile right, talk right, look right, and they hand you the keys to freedom. Literally. The man jiggled them in his pocket as he strode toward the uniform delivery van, taking tremendous satisfaction in the jangling sound they made.

He climbed into the van, tossing the clipboard with the morning's route on it in the back. *Sorry folks, change of plans.*

Cooks would go without their chef coats today, plumbers forced to plumb in their skivvies. And nurses would be sans cute little white getups. Now that'd be a pretty sight, wouldn't it?

The man grinned as he shifted gears, accelerating up the on-ramp for I-70 and Spector beyond.

But first, a quick pit stop.

Greta slept in an extra hour and then decided to go for one more. She had a lunch date with Jack Fenton, but that was still a few hours away.

She'd decided to give him another chance, see if those elusive sparks made an appearance after all. Besides, it would get her mother off her back about staying cooped up in the apartment.

Greta could hear her humming softly from her work-room as she finished up the last of the beadwork on the Mainbocher.

Good. The faster she was done with it, the faster Greta could get Gray Daniels out of her life permanently. Both him and his sweet, blushing bride.

On the nightstand, Greta's cell phone began vibrating. Again. She'd switched off the loud ringtone, but the phone rattled away almost constantly. Everyone on the planet seemed to be calling to express their condolences about the house.

And it was like that, wasn't it? Like someone had died.

A knock came at the door, and she heard her mother stir in her workroom. "I'll get it, Mom," Greta called. She got up and put on her robe.

She walked quietly up to the door and peered out through the peephole. Ian Koslovsky, his plump face red with excitement, pad and pencil in hand. No doubt ready to chronicle exactly how it felt when someone's entire life came tumbling down—literally—in one day. No thanks.

He knocked again and waited a full minute before at last turning away.

"Who was that?" Adele called from her workroom.

"No one. Just somebody at the wrong apartment."

Yawning, Greta headed into her room and climbed back into bed, not bothering to take off her robe. It was warm.

Greta pulled the covers up around her and nestled her head deep into the soft, fluffy pillow. Gosh, she felt like she could sleep all day long. Okay, clearly it was an es-cape mechanism, but she didn't care. It would pass after a while, right? Then she'd be able to face this enormous change in her and her mother's lives, figure out exactly what to do, come up with some sort of plan B.

"Darn it, Trina," the man muttered under his breath as he reached the end of the dirt driveway and stopped.

The truck was gone. His dad's old Chevy pickup. No doubt his sister had sold the darn thing and kept the money for herself. She better not try that with the house, assuming the old dump ever sold.

He let out a sharp breath in frustration. Now he'd have to stick with the van, as conspicuous as it was. He didn't know how to hotwire a car. Sure, he could've easily picked up that particular morsel of info the last couple of years. He'd been in the perfect place for it, after all. But he'd stayed pretty much to himself for the most part, happy just to get through each day unscathed.

Still, it should be okay. He figured he had a head start of about four hours before anyone noticed and raised the alarm.

He climbed out of the van and walked quickly along the side of the cabin to the storage shed in back, half jogging the last few yards. Yeah, he probably had nothing to worry about, but the hairs on the back of his neck still itched like he was being watched, paranoia setting in but good. He wanted to get the heck out of here, get moving.

Reaching the shed, he spotted the padlock on the door. Good lock, bad door. The wood along the bottom was ragged with rot. He kicked against it a couple of times and a crack split up the middle.

Heaving the two sections apart, he slid through the gap

into the shed. Good, all his dad's camping stuff was still here. Thankfully, Trina had never taken to the outdoors and so had left it alone. He started a pile in the middle of the floor. The tent and sleeping bags smelled a little musty, but they'd still do the trick.

He grabbed an old plastic milk crate and began filling it with anything he saw that might turn up useful during a long stay in the woods.

"Thanks a lot, old man," he muttered as he picked up the rusty old Coleman stove and added it to the pile. "Hope it's not too hot for you down there."

"Greta? I'm all done, Miss Sleepyhead." Her mother's singsong voice wafted down through thick folds of sleep. "Come and see! Come and see!"

Blinking her eyes awake, Greta dragged herself out of bed and padded into her mother's workroom.

Adele was standing proudly next to the dress form, the Mainbocher now fully restored, as stunning as the day it was created more than five decades earlier.

"I think we did a pretty good job, don't you?"

Greta nodded, circling the dress as she dredged up some measure of enthusiasm despite the blanket of sleepiness nearly overwhelming her.

When she'd worked up enough of a smile, at last she turned her gaze to her mother. "It's magnificent, Mom. I can just see Olivia de Havilland or Katharine Hepburn strolling grandly down the aisle in it."

"Oh, do you really think so?" her mother asked, beaming at the dress.

Greta stifled a yawn. "Absolutely. I'll go call Gray and let him know."

She went into her bedroom and sat down on the bed, feeling another yawn coming on. This time she didn't even try to stop it. Oh, to go back to sleep. But she couldn't. She had to start getting ready for her date with Jack. Maybe she should just cancel—*no*, she scolded herself. That would be giving in.

She'd better get some coffee in her, though, or her face might end up in her soup before the end of lunch.

Greta picked up her phone and scrolled down to Gray's name. And then, just as she pushed the SEND button, she felt it. Despite her fatigue and her futile self-denials, there it was. A spark. At the mere anticipation of hearing his voice.

So that was that. She'd fallen for a married man. Well, he'd be married soon enough anyway. She was almost glad when his voice mail kicked in.

Almost.

Chapter Twenty-three

So far, finalizing the seating chart for the reception was proving to be the single most unpleasant thing about the entire wedding ordeal. After a morning spent wrangling out a chart for the rest of the tables, only the head table was left. Besides his dad, Gray could care less who sat with them.

As it stood now, the table was nearly filled: Gray, Stephanie, Gray's dad, Stephanie's mom and her most recent husband, Stephanie's father and her longtime stepmother, and finally her grandfather. Only two seats left.

Unfortunately, Stephanie had three aunts, and they all wanted to sit at the head table. They'd spent days trying to jockey themselves into one of the coveted seats. Stephanie was on the phone now with the youngest aunt, Judy, apparently in tears.

Gray let out a breath and pulled out his phone to play a new game he'd downloaded onto it. Glancing at the screen, he saw the voice mail icon flashing and raised his eyebrows in surprise. He'd had his phone with him all morning. And then he remembered. He and Stephanie had gone to a movie last night and he'd neglected to turn the ringer back on.

He pressed the voice mail button and listened. One message. Greta Kendall. "Hi, I wanted to let you know the dress is ready. Sorry it took so long. With the move and everything . . ." Hearing her voice trail off, Gray frowned curiously. Did she sound nervous?

"Anyway, give me a call or have . . . your fiancée call me to schedule a fitting. I know there's only a couple of days before the wedding, but we'll have time to do any last-minute adjustments. Our docket's a little light at the moment." Gray winced at the bitter tone in those last words; her voice had been so soft at first. Still, he couldn't blame her.

He hung up and caught Stephanie's eye. "Your dress is ready," he whispered, not wanting to interrupt her call.

Her brows creased. "My dress?" she mouthed, but then Gray saw understanding clear in her eyes. She spoke then into the phone, but kept her eyes on Gray. "Sorry, Aunt Judy, I'm going to have to call you back."

She ended the call, put the phone down a little too carefully on the coffee table, and raised her blue eyes to meet his. "I meant to talk to you about that, darling. That dress."

Was that disdain in her voice? Yes, it came through in her expression also, her perfect little nose crinkling in the middle. "I'm not going to be wearing it."

Gray's lips parted in surprise. "But it's a tradition! And we promised my—"

But Stephanie cut him off, raising her hands in a placating gesture with just a touch of impatience. "Look, I *know* Mainbocher was a huge deal back then, and it's a great story about how your grandmother got it, but that was fifty years ago!"

And then she flashed him that full smile of hers, every

tooth present and accounted for. Years ago he'd named it her "news anchor" smile, perfect for segueing into a fluff piece after reporting on some horrific incident or another. "Now I'm starting a one-of-a-kind-custom-made-Vera-Wang-original tradition. Wait 'til you see it—it's spectacular! Vera really outdid herself. Cost a bloody fortune, but worth every penny."

Gray rose to his feet, spreading his hands wide in helpless frustration. "But we used to talk about it, how it would be. You were always so excited about wearing it."

"And then I grew up and got some fashion sense," Stephanie said matter-of-factly.

"It's not about *fashion*," Gray said and heard the pleading tone in the words. He cleared his throat. "It's about honoring the memories of my mother and my grandmother."

For a moment Stephanie just stared at him. As he saw the condescension settle in her blue eyes, he felt something unpleasant shift around in his heart.

She cocked her head to one side and thrust her lower lip out in a pout, but to Gray it only felt mocking. "Trust me, darling. It'll be beautiful, really. I'm sure they'd understand." She tossed him a careless, self-deprecating shrug. "And you know how clumsy I am. I'd probably have torn it or spilled something on it, and then where would we be?"

Gray stared at her for a long moment, his jaw stiffening as he realized exactly what this meant. "So it really was just a publicity stunt, taking the dress to Greta's shop." His voice was low and serious, but Stephanie didn't catch on.

"And it worked!" And then, unbelievably, Stephanie winked at him, trying to be cute.

Maybe a couple of months ago it would have worked on him. He would have laughed and pulled her into his arms. All forgiven.

But right now he could barely stand the sight of her.

"Why?" He'd spoken the word without thinking and was surprised at how calm and reasoned it sounded.

Stephanie again cocked her head, her perfectly plucked brows angled down in confusion. " 'Why' what?"

"Why am I marrying you?"

At that, something wavered in her eyes, fear perhaps, and the satisfaction it brought him didn't bode well for her.

But then Stephanie put on a pretend stern look, stood and walked up to him. She patted his cheek. "Because you asked me when we were six, and I said yes."

At the memory, Gray felt a smile tug at the sides of his mouth, the tightness of his jaw easing. "I thought you were the most beautiful thing I'd ever seen." He shook his head in remembered wonderment. "You were so perfect, like an angel. You used to take my breath away."

Now Stephanie shot one brow up in mock scolding. "Used to?"

Gray raised one shoulder in a bare, honest shrug. "Yes, *used* to."

"Not anymore?" Playfully, Stephanie planted her hands on her hips, a smile still hovering on her lips, but as he watched, it began to take on a forced quality. And there was that fear again, settling a little more firmly in the blue of her eyes.

Gray shook his head slowly. "No, not anymore."

He wasn't sure when the bulk of his love had drained

away, but it had, perhaps weeks ago, months maybe, leaving only a façade of love that he'd mistaken for the real thing. He shook his head, amazed at the realization. It had never occurred to him that it could happen, and so he'd never entertained the possibility. But now it was more than possibility. It was certainty.

His eyes flicked past her to the computer on her desk, and his mouth dropped open at what he saw there on the screen.

Two photos, side by side, both appearing at first glance to be the image Stephanie used to prove the post office in Willowby was the first one above ten thousand feet. But in the photo on the right, the sign above the door was just a little different.

Gray walked around Stephanie to get a better look. In the photo on the right, the sign clearly read BARBER SHOP, not POST OFFICE.

"You Photoshopped it." The words came out in a near whisper.

Now shame slid in beside the fear in Stephanie's eyes and she swallowed visibly. "Of course I did." She tossed him a too-careless shrug. "Well, I did the basics anyway, and then sent it to a guy I went to school with at D.U. who fixed the pixel edges, shadowing, and whatever else could give it away. By the time he was done, it would have passed any state-of-the-art analysis. Turned out it wasn't necessary. She didn't even bother to check it out. You know, I think I may have misjudged her tenacity."

"She couldn't afford an imaging expert," Gray said, his jaw set so tight he had to force the words through. He shook his head, slowly, controlled. "You know, it passed through my mind a couple of times that that's what you'd done, but I ignored it. I didn't think you'd stoop so low. Apparently I was wrong."

Gray narrowed his eyes. "The birth certificate, Bartland-Russell's, the one *I* used to defeat her in that landmark session. That was your work too, wasn't it?"

Stephanie's mouth turned down in a petulant frown. "No, not exactly."

He cocked his head at her. "Really."

Tears glistened in Stephanie's eyes, but she blinked them away. "That was all Anita Cox's idea. She did that part."

"But you did nothing to stop her. And you forced me to play a pivotal role in the little scheme the two of you hatched up."

Fresh shame coursed through Stephanie's eyes, and she let out a resigned breath. "I'm sorry."

Gray felt a muscle twitch in his jaw. "And so when the post office photo came up, you thought, what the hell, the line had already been crossed, why not do it again?"

Anger suddenly lanced through her eyes, wiping away both the shame and fear. "Look, whatever you may think of Winter's Haven, millions of dollars were—*are*—involved. You know how hard I worked to convince my father it would be worth it." She shook her head, hard and fierce. "I didn't have time for petty nostalgia. I've put everything on the line for this."

"But her *home* was on the line."

Stephanie flinched at the fury in the words, and fear made a return appearance in her eyes, taking a steady hold this time. And rightfully so.

"It's over, Stephanie," Gray said and was amazed how right the words felt to him. "I don't want to marry you anymore."

Her mouth dropped open. "What?"

"You heard me. I don't want to marry you."

Tears filled her beautiful, painfully familiar eyes, and unexpected guilt suddenly gnawed at him. "I'm sorry. I should have handled that differently."

He walked over to the desk, grabbed a tissue from the box, and brought it over to her. She took it automatically but made no move to wipe away the tears, leaving her cheeks wet, her mascara streaking down them. Guilt again tugged at Gray's heart.

"Look, I still love the little girl, but I'm having a hard time with the woman she's turned into." Stephanie said nothing, but only stared at him in stunned disbelief, tears streaming down her face.

He took a step closer to her. "You've changed, Stephanie," he said softly. "This mall has changed you. It made you hard and mean. I used to chalk it up to your being so very desperate to impress your father, to show him you'd grown up into a strong woman. But now I think it was already there, had *always* been there, and Winter's Haven only brought it to the forefront."

"But I could change back," she said, her voice hitching on the words, "be that little gir—"

But Gray found himself shaking his head. "I'm sorry, Stephanie, it's too late now. I . . . can't love you anymore."

Stephanie winced as if he'd slapped her. And yes, he felt bad about that, but at the same time, saying the words out loud felt incredibly liberating, like a heavy burden had been lifted from his chest.

And with that came a realization. He did love some-one, didn't he? Or was certainly starting to. Even after only a few weeks.

Perhaps he'd known that very first day back in her shop.

Chapter Twenty-four

Gray probably broke about a dozen traffic laws getting to Greta Kendall's apartment, but so what? He would've gladly paid any ticket he got and kept the receipt as a souvenir of the day.

He parked in the visitor's lot, climbed out of the truck. and jogged across the street to her door. He knocked and waited. Nothing.

A shuffling noise came from the other side of the door. "Greta? Greta, it's Gray."

The doorknob remained still, but again he thought he heard something brush against the door.

"I hear you in there! Please, I need to talk to you." He pressed his palms against the door, willing it to open.

At last her voice came from inside, low and tense. "I told you to call to schedule a—"

"Oh, never mind that," he cut in. "It's something else. Something important I have to tell you."

Gray let out a breath. This was not going at all how he'd envisioned.

"Please, Greta. Just open the door."

Something in his voice made her change her mind, something soft and pleading and desperate.

Greta unlocked the door and opened it cautiously. Gray wore jeans and a black T-shirt that, together with his dark lashes, intensified the blue of his eyes. His hair was tousled, as if he'd been raking his fingers through it over and over again. She hadn't seen him in nearly two weeks and had forgotten just how gorgeous he was. Just the sight of him made her heart race in her chest.

"Hi," he said with an odd little smile.

Greta swallowed hard before speaking. "Look, I'm not sure why you're here, but—"

"Please, Greta, just hear me out, okay? Can I come in?"

"I don't think that's a good idea."

"Please?"

That weird half grin was still on his face, damn him. Anger rippled through her. "I went by the house yesterday, you know. It's gone. It's really gone."

Unbelievably, Gray's face split into a wide-open smile. "Well, of course it is."

Anger blossomed into rage, and before Greta knew it, her hand was in the air ready to slap him across the face, make him feel some of the pain she'd suffered the last few weeks.

But Gray stopped her arm mid-arc, grabbing her elbow. He held on firmly, though not enough to hurt her.

At least the smile was gone.

"Will you listen to me? Please?"

Greta yanked her arm away and rubbed her elbow, mostly to wipe away the array of tingles that had erupted there from his touch. "What, you want one last fling before you tie the knot? Sorry, I've got plans today."

For a moment he just looked at her, his jaw set, frustration and anger alternating vividly in his eyes. But was there something else in there too? "Look, I— Well, the last few weeks I've . . ." Gray stopped, huffed out a breath, and swiped both hands through his hair, hard. "Oh, never mind."

And then he was slipping his hands around her waist and pulling her toward him, his face angling down toward hers.

The idea of turning away from him flitted through her mind, but vanished just as quickly. Instead, Greta's lips parted as Gray leaned in closer, and then those lips were pressing down on her own, just as she'd imagined that very first day back in her shop. Smooth, firm, powerful.

There was tension in them at first, but as the kiss deepened, Gray's lips softened and began working masterfully against hers. Still, there was an urgency to it.

So then, one last kiss before tying the knot.

The second that thought reared its ugly head, Greta jerked back away from Gray, her mouth throbbing and tingling.

"Am I interrupting something?"

It was Jack, walking up from the street. How much had he seen? Enough, Greta realized, seeing his heavy scowl.

"No, you're not," she said, still a little breathless. She glowered at Gray. "*He* was." She managed a smile for Jack as she turned away from Gray. "Come on, let's go." She took a step toward the door. "Mom?" she called inside. "We're leaving for lunch."

Adele came to the door holding a teacup. When she

saw both Gray and Jack standing there, confusion passed through her brown eyes. "Oh, hello, boys."

"Bye, Mom." Greta kissed her mother's cheek.

"Good-bye, dear."

She again worked up a smile as she touched Jack's arm. "Ready?" He nodded, his face rigid.

"Wait, Greta—" Gray began, taking a step toward her, but Jack stepped in front of him, his eyes glowering.

"When she said 'we're leaving,' she didn't mean you. Isn't that right, Greta?"

Greta nodded and turned away from Gray, avoiding any eye contact with him, afraid of what she'd see simmering in those blue eyes.

As they headed toward his Bronco, Greta heard her mom from behind her. "I was just about to have a little lunch, Gray. Won't you join me? I'd love the company."

"Thanks," Greta heard him respond, his voice gruff. "I'd like that."

Wonderful. He'd better be gone by the time she got back.

Chapter Twenty-five

She's just so unhappy right now," Adele said, stirring some cream into her tea. They were seated in the apartment's sad little kitchen, the red design in the wallpaper faded to near pink. Thank God it was only temporary.

Gray remembered Greta's smile as she walked off with Fenton, her curls loose around her shoulders. She'd been wearing a dress he hadn't seen before, a short ruffled number that showed off her legs.

He couldn't stifle a bitter grunt. "She seemed happy enough going out with Jack Fenton today."

"Exactly," Adele said with a perfunctory nod. "*Seemed* happy. For your benefit. And mine. I've been nagging at her to get out of the house. But happy? I don't think so." She took a sip of tea. "The last time I really saw her happy was that morning when I made pancakes. With you."

Gray saw a small smile play on her lips at the memory. He felt himself grinning as well. "I haven't seen that light in her eyes in a very long time." Adele's smiled faded. "She's in a bad place, Gray. She's been avoiding contact with everyone, not answering the door, turning the ringer off on her phone. Sometimes the way she looks at me makes me feel like she wishes I were gone too, like I'm a burden she has to bear."

Tears brimmed in her eyes but she blinked them away. "I don't think she even realizes how depressed she is. She tried to put on a good show in Denver, but I could see. All she wants to do now is sleep. She's not eating right either. She's lost at least five pounds in the last couple of weeks." Her lips thinned into a hard line. "It's like how she was with Mark."

"Her ex?" Gray's throat constricted at the very thought of him.

Adele nodded, stark pain radiating in her eyes. "Yes. He hurt her so badly. Both physically and emotionally." She shuddered. "The bruises. She tried to hide them from me, but twice I saw the imprint of his fingers on her arm."

As the image of that flashed vividly in his mind, Gray felt his shoulders become rigid with rage. Tears again swam in Adele's deep brown eyes, and this time a stream of them trailed down her cheeks. She swiped them away angrily.

"Do you have any idea how it felt to see my own daughter hurt like that? And there wasn't a blasted thing I could do about it. She was blind to it for so long. 'It was just one time, Mom,' she'd say."

Adele shook her head in remembered frustration. "It took his breaking her wrist for it to finally sink in."

Hearing that, Gray's fingers clenched around his tea-cup so hard he realized the fragile porcelain was in danger of shattering. He loosened his grip, but his jaw, his shoulders, remained tense. He looked again at Adele, and saw she was shaking her head as she relived what must have been a horrific time for her. "Even then I had to convince her to press charges. Thank God the rat's in jail now."

She took a sip of tea and then let out a long breath seeped

in regret. "This is probably all my fault. I didn't encourage her to move on after that. I wanted her to stay close. I wanted to protect her. And so the shop, the house, was all she had."

At that, Gray frowned. "But—" He stopped as it finally dawned on him. And here he'd been thinking Greta was depressed over *him*. Something his mother said to him when he was being a selfish kid came back to him. *The world doesn't revolve around you, Gray Daniels.*

He leaned forward, his eyes riveted on Adele. "You said she hasn't been answering anyone's calls." She shook her head. "Has she been listening to her messages?"

Again, Adele shook her head. "She says she'll listen to them when she's ready, when—" She stopped when she saw the smile break over his face. Her thin brows furrowed in confusion that only deepened when Gray suddenly stood up and held out his hand.

"Come with me, dear lady. There's something you need to see."

Chapter Twenty-six

At least Gray was gone. Greta didn't think she could deal with him right now. Or how she felt about him.

"Mom?" she called out, setting her purse down on the coffee table. "I'm back."

Silence.

"Mom?"

Frowning, Greta strode to her mother's room, found it empty. The familiar dread took hold in her heart.

A knock came at the door, and she rushed back over to it. Maybe someone had found Adele wandering somewhere and brought her home.

"Mom?" Greta said as she yanked open the door. But then she just stood there stunned, staring in disbelief. She actually blinked a couple of times to make sure her mind wasn't playing tricks on her.

Mark Kendall stood in front of her, his mouth split in a wide smile, the dimples on either side on full display.

"Mark?"

He nodded once, his green eyes sparkling. "In the flesh."

His hair was shorter than she'd remembered. He'd always been so vain about it, his long, thick blond hair. He looked thinner too, and unnaturally pale.

He wore a generic-looking maintenance uniform, JASON written in blue script across the left side pocket.

"But how—"

Mark let out a dark chuckle. "Oh, I played nice, and they let me into a work-release program. Good behavior and all that."

One side of his mouth turned up in an all too familiar half smile, smug and just a little menacing. "I can be *very* nice when I want to be. I'm sure you remember that, don't you, babe?"

Oh, yes, she remembered.

"So this morning I decided to take a little break. I wanted to see you."

Greta swallowed hard, trying to squash the panicky scream that kept bubbling up. "So how did you find me?"

Mark shrugged. "I saw your house was gone, so I asked around." He let out a contemptuous snort. "People in small towns are so dang trusting. So, you going to invite me in or what?"

Greta hesitated, her gaze sweeping across the front of the building. There was no one around, no one to help her.

Mark cocked his head in a jaunty way she had once found incredibly charming. "Come on, darlin', you're hurting my feelings here." Without waiting for an answer, he brushed past her and into the apartment.

Greta looked around again before closing the door. Her heart was pounding hard in her chest, and her whole body felt a little shaky. She drew in a deep, calming breath and let it out, slow and controlled. She needed to keep her wits about her. Turning to face him, she worked up a neutral expression. It was the best she could do.

"I wanted to deliver the last one in person."

Mark pulled his right arm from behind his back and raised a photograph up to her. Their wedding. The twelfth eight-by-ten.

Greta took in the picture, the cheap dress, that haunted cast to her eyes, his self-satisfied smile.

Mark took a step closer to her, and Greta willed herself to not back away. Right now she needed to keep him calm, to go along with whatever he said or did. It would give her time to think.

"See? I told you we'd be together again." Grinning, Mark lifted his hand to her face, and Greta jerked back instinctively, unable to control it. She sucked in a quick breath, afraid of his reaction. But he only pulled his hand away and nodded, his mouth forming a tight line, seemingly of regret.

"I don't blame you one bit for that. Not one bit." She saw his eyes soften as he took in her face, his gaze roaming over every inch. "You are so damn beautiful." This time she didn't flinch as he raised his hand and gently brushed the back of his fingers down her cheek. A shudder threatened at the feel of his flesh against hers, but she squelched it. Hopefully her expression didn't give her away.

"Come sit with me, okay?" Taking her hand, Mark drew her over to the couch and sat down beside her. He took in a long breath and let it out.

"Now, look, I know I made some mistakes. God knows I've had time to think about every last one of them. It won't happen again, none of it. I promise you." He gave her a small, sheepish smile, just the sides of his mouth curving up. "I took an anger-management class they offered, just like you always wanted me to. I even got a certificate."

His smile slowly fell away. "I love you, Greta. I really do. And I know somewhere inside there you still love me." He squeezed her hand. "We had something good, didn't we? Real good."

Greta found herself nodding automatically and instantly felt the shame in it, giving in to him after all this time. She couldn't get him riled up, though, not now when she was finally thinking more clearly, her initial blind panic ebbing away.

"Thing is, though, my break time's about to run out, and I can't see going back just yet. I thought it'd be nice for us to go away, just the two of us. Maybe a little camping trip, give us a chance to get reacquainted, while I figure out what the heck to do next. What do you think?"

Mark lifted his hand to grasp a curl that had fallen out of her ponytail. He let it slip through his fingers all the way down to the end.

"And don't you worry your pretty little head about being cold at night. You'll have me to cuddle up next to, of course. And I stopped by my dad's place on the way up and picked up all his camping gear."

His dad had a small house just outside the town of Genesee in the foothills above Denver. Mark smirked. "He won't be missing it. He died last year, you know. While I was inside. I didn't even get to say good-bye to him. Boo-hoo for me."

His sarcasm came through loud and clear, and Greta couldn't blame him. His father had beaten Mark nearly every day of his young life, turning him into this monster.

"Oh, Mark, I don't know. My mother—"

"Yeah, good old Adele." Something cold and hard slithered through his eyes, something that scared Greta badly. "I know she put you up to it, testifying against me, divorcing me. And I bet she's why you didn't visit me, not once. Am I right?"

Holding her gaze, Mark angled his head, a small indefinable smile ghosting across his lips. Greta wasn't sure if he was being serious or sarcastic. She remembered the feeling well, not knowing if he was Nice Mark or Mean Mark only acting nice. God forbid she guessed wrong.

She nodded and again felt that flash of shame.

"I thought so. Where is the old bat anyway?"

"I'm not sure." Hopefully far, far away.

"All right then, let's blow before she gets back." Mark let go of Greta's hand, patted her knee, and stood up. "We should pack up some things before we go—food, clothes. And you'll probably want to change." He glanced down at her dress, the one she'd worn for her disastrous lunch date with Jack. Gosh, it seemed like a million years ago. "Shame, though. That dress sure does something nice to those legs of yours."

Chapter Twenty-seven

Greta went into the bathroom to change. And to think. Outside the door, she heard him first in the kitchen, opening and closing the refrigerator and cabinets, the thuds and clinks of cans as he tossed them into a box, the tinkle of silverware. Then he moved into her room and she heard drawers being opened and slammed shut as he packed up some of her clothes.

Glancing in the mirror over the sink, Greta saw the bleakness in her eyes. She'd thought this part of her life was over. But no, here was the helplessness again, the weakness, the feeling of being absolutely conquered and so very alone.

And God only knew where her mother was. Hopefully she wouldn't come back while Mark was here. Greta wanted absolutely no contact between Adele and this psychopath.

What was she going to do? *Hurry,* came the immediate answer. Her mother could come to her senses wherever she was and come back home at any moment.

Greta wished she knew how long it would be before someone noticed Mark had bolted from work-release and she was discovered to be missing. Would a search party be formed? Still, Mark and Greta would get a head start, and Mark knew these mountains. But at least her mother would be safe. She'd figure something else out later.

God help her, if she did get out of this situation, she would never allow this to happen again, never let herself become this vulnerable. Never.

Quickly, Greta slipped the dress off and tugged on a pair of capris and a T-shirt, and then slid on a pair of sneakers.

She came out of the bathroom and found Mark just outside the door holding her duffel bag. "Don't forget your toothbrush, darlin'." Again, one side of his mouth curled up in that scary half grin. "We wouldn't want you getting any cavities out there, now, would we?"

Her jaw set, Greta ducked back inside the bathroom and grabbed some basic toiletry items. She was stuffing them into the side pocket of the duffel when a knock came at the front door.

Instantly, Mark's entire body went tense, and he let the duffel bag drop to the floor with a loud thump.

He went to the door and looked through the peephole. "It's some guy. You expecting someone?" Greta saw jealousy harden Mark's eyes into cold emeralds.

Greta shook her head, trying for innocence. "No. Let me see."

He moved aside, and Greta peered through the little hole.

Gray.

For half a second she thought about calling out to him for help. But no, she couldn't risk his getting hurt. This was her problem.

"Greta? I hear you in there." Even through the door she

heard Gray heave out a sigh. "Look, I've got a couple of things to say to you, and I'm not leaving here until I do."

Mark let out a breath. "Who *is* this guy?"

"Nobody," Greta said nonchalantly. "I helped his fiancée with her wedding dress, that's all."

Mark's brows lifted in dubious surprise. "Really."

"Yeah. That's probably why he's here. He's getting married on Saturday and needs the dress."

Mark grabbed her upper arm, and Greta felt jealousy tighten his grip painfully around her arm, his fingers biting into her flesh.

"You sure that's all he is to you? Sounds a little more . . . intense than that to me." He shook his head. "Either way, I want you to get rid of him." He looked around and spotted the water heater closet in the hallway. "I'm just here working on the water heater, got it?"

Greta nodded, swallowed hard, and walked up to the door.

Chapter Twenty-eight

Greta swung open the door, an odd, forced-looking smile on her face. "Hello, Gray," she said stiffly, almost formal. But that was understandable. She was angry about that kiss he'd stolen earlier, wasn't she?

"Look, Greta—"

"Wait here," she cut in. "I'll go and get the dress."

The dress? Oh, right. She still thought he was getting married on Saturday. No wonder she was so mad. He needed to get this all sorted out and fast.

"Greta, I—" Gray began, but she was already striding fast toward the hallway. But maybe that was a good thing. He hadn't figured out exactly what to say to her, and he didn't want to flub it.

He spotted the man working on the water heater and frowned. Darn it, he didn't want an audience for what he had to say. Maybe they could go outside.

"Howdy," the man said.

"Hey."

The man, Jason, his shirt read, grinned. "So you're gettin' hitched, huh? That's great. Just great. I was married once. Best time of my life."

Gray nodded noncommittally, and the man turned his attention back to the water heater.

Greta came back into the room holding the Mainbocher tucked away in the bag.

"Look, Greta, could we go outside and—" But as she approached him, she held up the dress, and the sleeve of her T-shirt rode up a couple of inches. Was that—yes, bright red impressions of fingers, all in a row. And fresh.

"What happened to your—" He stopped when he saw the maintenance man behind her suddenly straighten, his good-old-boy smile gone, replaced by something dark and menacing. Greta turned and saw the man coming.

And then time seemed to switch into overdrive. Greta whirled back around, thrust the dress bag into Gray's arms, and began pushing him hard toward the door. Gray was so surprised at this sudden turn of events that, for a moment, he just let it happen.

But then he saw the hammer in the man's hand as he came up behind Greta. "There you go, Mr. Daniels." Greta was clearly aiming for casual and cordial, but missed the mark by a mile. Instead, panic and fear drove through every syllable. "I hope everything goes well. Bye now."

"Wait," Gray protested, but he was talking to a closed door. The dead bolt clicked in place. There was something damning about the sound. Final.

His heart hammering against his ribs, Gray forced himself to stop panicking and just think for a moment. Greta was in danger, and he couldn't get back inside to help her. The police.

He reached into his pocket for his cell phone, but remembered it was on the charger in his truck. It occurred to him then that it might actually be a good thing for her if he made it seem like everything was okay for now, that he hadn't recognized Mark Kendall or the impression of his hand on Greta's arm. He'd be just a groom hurrying off with his bride's dress.

Without glancing back at the door, he started down the path toward his truck across the street.

Mark squinted through the peephole. "Okay, he's leaving."

Turning away from the door, he grabbed Greta once again by the upper arm, and she cringed. Why did he always go for the same exact spot? "All right, let's go. I want to get the heck out of Dodge."

"Okay, okay," Greta said, nearly tripping over the duffel bag in the hallway as she tried to keep up with his long, fast strides.

In the kitchen, Mark hefted the box of supplies up under one arm and then tugged Greta back down the hall.

"Pick that up," he ordered, nodding down at the duffel. Greta bent down and grabbed it, aware she was quickly running out of options. As if she'd ever really had any.

Mark yanked her over to the door and then paused to flash her that mean half grin one more time. "Be a good girl now and just walk quietly over to the van. Got it? Now open the door."

Greta unlocked the dead bolt and swung open the door. Instantly her eyes cut across the street to the visitor's lot. Gray's truck was still there. Oh, God, she hoped he didn't try anything. *Just call the police*, she silently begged him.

She saw the dark shape of him behind the wheel and felt his eyes on her as Mark led her over to a uniform-delivery van parked in front of the apartment.

Greta opened the sliding door and climbed in. "We're

going to have to ditch this thing ASAP," Mark mumbled as he jumped in behind her. He set the box down by the door. "Now get in the back."

The van was filled with dozens of bundles of folded uniforms bound by plastic ties. Greta looked around to see if there was anything she could use to get out of this situation.

The camping gear was piled up in a back corner—a tent, sleeping bags, a Coleman stove, and a milk crate filled with cooking utensils, a lantern, flashlights, and some other camping basics. There had to be a knife in there somewhere.

Greta sat down on a bundle close to the pile. Maybe while he was driving she could move the box closer with her foot and surreptitiously look through it. She wasn't sure what she would do even if she did get her hands on a knife, but at least it would be something, a glimmer of hope.

Chapter Twenty-nine

Gray watched in dismay as Kendall closed the sliding door of the van. The police weren't going to get here in time. He had to make a move. Right now.

He couldn't let them leave. The second Kendall saw the police coming, he'd take off fast and maybe crash with Greta in the van. Or he'd get away and disappear into the mountains, and Gray would never see Greta again.

Both options were unacceptable. His heart thundering in his chest, Gray put the truck in reverse and backed up.

Mark turned the key in the ignition, and the engine rumbled to life. "What the hell?" Greta heard him mutter. She looked up to see Gray's truck squeal to a stop in front of them, blocking the way. Gray got out and slammed the door behind him.

Mark unrolled the window. "Whatcha doing there, friend?"

"Stopping you." Tears brimmed in Greta's eyes when she heard the resolve in Gray's voice. She wasn't alone in this after all, was she? "And now you're going to get out of the van."

"Oh, really," Mark scoffed. "And who's going to make me? You, pretty boy?"

Craning her neck, Greta saw Gray walk around to the

driver's-side door, determination resonating in his dark eyes.

Suddenly, Mark swung the van door open hard and fast, ramming it against Gray's forehead. It made a terrible dull *thunk* as it connected. Greta sucked in air. No!

She watched in horror as Gray lurched sideways and then stumbled blindly in front of the van. Without even thinking about it, Greta headed for the sliding door and fumbled with the latch.

"And just where do you think you're going, little missy?"

Mark stood, leaned over, and grabbed her yet again by her upper arm, yanking her away from the door. Greta winced, but this time the pain had a different effect on her. Gone were the fear and helplessness.

Instead, rage, deep and cold, swept through her. She was done with this man causing her pain. She would be his victim not one moment longer. For way too long she'd allowed him to get to her, keep her down, even from inside prison. No more.

Her jaw set, Greta turned her gaze on him, his handsome features contorted into an ugly scowl. "I'm going to see if he's all right." She was pleased to hear the calm assurance in her voice.

"Oh, no you're not."

She ripped her arm away from him and was surprised how easy it had been. She'd never tried that before, and Mark gaped at her now as if he suddenly had no clue who she was. And he didn't. "Yes. I am." She headed back over to the door, grabbed the latch, and slid it open.

Furious, Mark jumped back into the driver's seat. "I swear I'll run you over. Both of you."

Greta looked directly into his eyes, eyes she'd once loved so very much, piercing vivid green, almond-shaped, surrounded by lush dark lashes. But now she saw fear hovering in the edges of them, little-boy fear echoing back to the time when his innocence was so brutally beaten away. He was in over his head here and knew it. Now she did too.

"No, you won't," she said and was stunned by how simple it sounded, yet the truth of it reverberated all around them. She turned, jumped down out of the van, and flew around to the front.

Gray was leaning against the van, breathing fast and hard, his eyes unfocused as he tried to stand up fully. "It's okay," Greta murmured. "I've got you now."

She slipped her shoulder beneath his arm and, supporting his weight, got him over to the grass by the sidewalk.

Glancing up at the cab of the van, she saw Mark just watching them, dazed disbelief in his eyes.

Tires screeched behind her, and Greta looked back to see an SUV careening around the corner, red and blue lights flashing.

The sight of it seemed to spur Mark back into action, and he began backing up, the van making loud, slow beeps as he maneuvered his way out of the parking spot.

Suddenly another police-marked SUV roared up behind it, blocking any further escape. Greta looked up and saw Mark mouth a curse and then raise his arms in surrender.

It was over.

Liam Shaw jumped out of the first SUV and ran up to them. "Greta? Are you all—"

"I'm fine." She nodded down at Gray. "He's not, though."

Liam nodded and signaled to the paramedics that were racing up the street.

"I have to find my mother," Greta said. "Can you—"

"She's fine." Gray had said the words. Greta looked at him and was happy to see his eyes clearing and able to focus. But how would he know about her mother?

"Come on, I'll take you to her." Gray struggled to stand up but needed Greta and Liam's help.

Liam frowned. "Shouldn't you get your head checked out?"

"Later." Gray smiled at Greta. "Right now there's something I'd much rather do."

Chapter Thirty

Even though his senses seemed to have fully returned, Gray let Greta drive. "Turn here," he said, and Greta frowned as she turned onto South Willow.

"But how did you know where she was?"

He flashed her a teasing smile. "Because I brought her here. And she wouldn't leave, just told me to come get you."

"But why—"

Greta stopped the truck with a jerk, gulping in air, her eyes nearly bugging out of her skull as they arrived at the familiar meadow. Although it was no longer empty.

There sat the Gingerbread House, completely intact, the warm brown paint gleaming in the afternoon sun. Greta closed her eyes and then opened them again. It was still there.

It looked completely at home, as if it had always wanted to be there, a seamless fit, the mountains soaring majestically behind it. She'd be able to hear the brook running through the backyard from the side window of her bedroom.

And then the house blurred as tears filled her eyes. "You did this, didn't you?"

Gray shrugged. "It wasn't too hard. I did a little research in the town archives, found the site of the fire, and then looked into the old county deeds, saw your grandfather's name. Turns out your family still owns it. Then I hired a company that specializes in— Oh, come on, now." He stopped as she began sobbing in earnest, and pulled her into his arms.

"So my mom's here?" Greta asked, when she could finally talk again. But then her question was answered when she saw Adele happily waving at them through the bay window in her old room.

"My room. I never thought I'd see it again."

More tears brimmed and trickled down her cheeks. Chuckling softly, Gray wiped them away with his thumbs. "Come on, let's go inside."

Unable to speak, Greta only nodded and got out of the truck. And then she let out a delighted little laugh through her tears.

There was the old pathway, transported here brick by brick, complete with new peppermint twist phlox planted along either side. Young plants still with wide spaces between them. But they'd grow. By this time next year, they'd fill in and bloom the solid masses of pink she loved so much.

Greta shook her head in slow wonder. It all seemed so surreal. She tore her gaze away from the house to look back at Gray. "But why? Why would you do this for us?"

A small, puzzled smile grazed his lips. "Don't you know?"

Greta shook her head, but as Gray's smile faded, the blue of his eyes darkening close to black, she did know. Still, hearing the words out loud sent fresh tingles surging through her belly. "I care about you, Greta. That's why."

"But what about Stephanie?"

"It's over. It had been for a while, I think. I just didn't realize it." Gray lifted one shoulder in a half shrug. "I think I mistook familiarity for love. Now I know the difference." He reached up and cradled Greta's face in his hands. "Now I know what it's like to really start falling in love with someone." He grinned. "That's you, by the way."

And then he was leaning in to kiss her, and this time his lips moved much more slowly than before, gentle and tender against hers, with no trace of the urgent desperation of their first kiss. Oh, yes, this one took its time.

For a moment, Greta let herself fall into the kiss, allowed it to saturate her entire being as she tasted the fledgling love on his lips, her own soaring up to meet his in a perfect match. But then she pulled back. Gray's hands fell away from her face, and she felt the sudden cold void there. But it couldn't be helped.

"I can't, Gray. I'm sorry."

The puzzlement returned to his eyes, but now she saw fear glimmering behind them too.

Greta shook her head as she struggled for the right words. "Seeing Mark again, going through that, made me more determined than ever never to be in that situation again."

Gray clasped her elbow, squeezed it. "But he's gone. He's going back to jail. You beat him. *You* beat him."

Greta nodded. "Yes, but it doesn't change how I feel about this." She looked up at him, his beautiful face going watery as fresh tears brimmed in her eyes, no longer happy ones.

"You don't know, Gray. You can't know how it was. I was

so in love with him, so completely in love. It made me blind. I knew it was coming, felt it building up, yet I stayed. I let him, *allowed* him to hurt me. And I went right back for more. I'd listen to his pleas and reassurances, believe them. 'The last time, the last time,' he'd say. And I went back. I went *back*." She swiped at her tears angrily with the heels her palms.

"I'd hear my mom and dad say 'get away,' and sometimes I'd actually listen." She smiled but felt the darkness in it. "In those moments, just those moments, I really *heard* them and I'd see Mark for who—*what* he was. But then he'd look at me with those pretty green eyes of his, and I'd melt under them and reality would go away again."

She looked at Gray, directly into his eyes, willing him to understand. "Do you hear what I'm saying? Love made me lose myself, my judgment. I wasn't in control. And now I have those feelings with you, or the beginnings of them anyway."

Gray's features looked suddenly ravaged. "You don't think— Greta, do you think *I'd* hurt you? That I could *ever* hurt you?" Greta saw the naked pain behind the words, and it wrenched at her insides to see it.

"I don't know!" She'd shouted the words and glanced up to see Adele looking out at them, concerned, through the bay window on the first floor now. Greta managed a weak smile and a wave to show her everything was fine. Just fine.

"I don't know that you would," she said, her voice soft with tension. "I also don't know for sure you wouldn't."

Gray swept a hand through his hair. "But *I* know. I'm asking you to trust that."

Greta heaved out a breath. "You don't get it. I don't trust *myself.* I trusted my decisions before and look where it got me. I can't take the chance it'll happen again. I won't let myself. I need you to respect that."

He took a step toward her and looked devastated when she jerked back away from him. "Please, Greta. Don't cut me off like this. I get that you're afraid. I understand that. Let's just take it slow, see if you *do* become sure. And if you don't, I'll go."

Greta felt her shoulders droop, her defenses weakening. Now that the adrenaline was finally wearing off, emotional exhaustion began settling in fast. "I don't know, Gray. I feel so . . . damaged."

"So why don't you give yourself a chance to heal? And give me a chance to help you?"

Greta hesitated, considering. "We'll take it slow?"

"As slow as you need to. It's in your hands." Gray took another step toward her, and this time she didn't move away. "Please, Greta. Give me—*us*—a chance."

She studied his face for a long moment, saw the sincerity and pleading in his eyes. "Okay."

His lips parted in a tentative smile. "Okay?"

"Yes."

He heaved out a huge sigh. "Good. *Now* can we go inside?"

Greta nodded and Gray grasped her hand and looked down at it. "Is this all right?"

She smiled. "It's fine."

But as they walked up the pathway, Greta felt her smile slip away. Was she doing the right thing here?

Only time would tell.

Chapter Thirty-one

Greta and her mother spent one last night in the cramped apartment. Their furniture was still there. But Gray said he'd come over in the morning to help move at least some of their stuff back into the Gingerbread House. How wonderful it would be to sleep in her old room again.

With a sigh, Greta plopped down on her bed and grabbed her phone from the nightstand. She should have been happier than she was, wished she could have just given into her feelings for Gray without a glance back. But she couldn't. Having the house back would just have to do.

She dialed into her voice mail and began listening to the messages from the last couple of weeks. She'd been so wrong. Not one of them was offering condolences about the house, only congratulations on its being saved. So many familiar voices.

But then Greta frowned as a voice came on she didn't recognize. "Hello, Ms. Kendall, my name is Adam Harwood, Stephanie Harwood's father." Greta's brows winged up in surprise. "I just wanted to tell you how glad I was to hear about the house being moved."

He chuckled, sounding self-conscious. "I'm sorry my feeble attempts at helping you proved so fruitless. I'm also sorry for the subterfuge in sneaking them into your mailbox as I did."

Greta's mouth dropped open in shock. Adam Harwood was her mysterious benefactor?

"Obviously, I didn't want my daughter finding out. Her heart was so set on that blasted mall." Greta heard him sigh into the phone. "I now know why she was so adamant about it. My wife Connie brought it to my attention recently that somewhere along the line, while I wasn't looking, my little girl had grown up. The poor thing was just trying to show me she was now a woman, a savvy businesswoman at that. Maybe if I'd realized that sooner, all those old houses would still be standing."

He chuckled into the phone. "I've discovered after more than seven decades on this planet I appreciate more the . . . oldness of things, that they should be treasured, valued. And now, thankfully, at least one piece of the past has been saved. I'm so very happy for you. Take care now."

Greta shook her head, amazed. How incredibly ironic that Stephanie had been working so hard to please her father, when he'd been the one trying to sabotage her!

The last message was from the Colorado Department of Corrections, warning her about Mark walking away from his work-release program.

"Thanks, guys," Greta said wryly and hung up the phone.

Chapter Thirty-two

Gray was quiet through dinner. They were at a new Cuban place in Aspen, celebrating the closing of the sale of his father's house. It had taken three months to sell, the tough real estate market taking its toll even in Aspen. Although he was glad to have finally sold it, Greta knew it was bittersweet for him, letting go of his childhood home, and so she didn't push conversation on him.

The waiter brought them coffee, and Gray seemed to take his time stirring in sugar and cream. Too much time. Greta saw the side of his cheek pucker and knew he was chewing the inside of it. Was something more going on here than the house?

"I got a job offer yesterday," he said, his eyes still on the coffee.

Greta felt her stomach muscles instantly constrict. "Really? That's great." But she heard the hollowness in the words. She already knew where this was going.

"It's in San Diego."

"Oh. I see."

Now Gray did look up from his coffee, and Greta saw a thousand different emotions roiling in his eyes. "A new firm looking for someone with fresh ideas. They liked my design for Winter's Haven. And I found a great place for my dad, right by the beach."

Greta's brows drew together as she realized he'd known about this for a while, had probably sent the plans in himself for their consideration. Tears prickled the back of her eyes, and she blinked hard to keep them at bay. Some part of her had known this was coming. She'd been living on borrowed time with Gray the last three months and darn well knew it. So why did she feel so blindsided?

Because he'd given up on her. The thought felt like a punch to her gut. And how utterly absurd of her to feel that way.

Gray had been so sure her feelings would change, that her memories of that horrible day with Mark would fade and she'd come to accept his love. But Gray didn't understand how much it meant to her, the vow she'd made to the terrified Greta in that bathroom. Breaking it, allowing herself to become blinded by love once again, losing herself in it, would be like betraying that part of her. And she would not do that.

Still, it had been selfish of her to keep him here, and had been from the start. She should have ended it long before this, convinced him it wasn't going to happen between them. And yet she'd been unable to do it, couldn't make herself say the words.

Gray reached over to cradle her hand gently in his. Now it was she who kept her eyes on the coffee in front of her, avoiding what she knew would be shimmering in his eyes.

"I really do love you, Greta."

Greta closed her eyes as tears welled. "I'm sorry."

She heard his quick intake of air as his hand pulled away. Greta opened her eyes to see his palm splayed flat on the table, his fingertips grinding into the tablecloth, bunching up the fabric. "I don't want you to be sorry. I want—" He leaned back in his chair and raked a hand through his hair.

He looked around the room, and Greta saw tears in his eyes now too. "I have to get out of here," he said, the words hoarse and strained. "Please, can we leave?"

Her stomach uncomfortably tight, Greta nodded and stood up, wiping tears off her own cheeks as Gray yanked out his wallet and threw cash down on the table.

They didn't say a word to each other the entire way back up to Spector, both only mumbling "Good night" when she got out. At least they'd avoided the sticky question of the good-night kiss.

He never made a move for one, allowing Greta to set the pace for whatever it was they'd been doing. She'd tried hard to keep things light between them, nearly platonic. And yet several times during the last three months, she'd leaned over and pressed her lips against his without even thinking about it. It had just felt so right. But then she'd remember. And each time, she'd pull away quickly and hurry out of his truck, not wanting to see the desire, the love, she suspected she would find in his eyes.

Afterwards, she'd swear to herself not to do it again, that it was unfair to him. She'd never been a tease and didn't want to start now. She respected Gray far too much for that. And yet, despite herself, a couple of weeks later, there'd she be again, finding his lips warm and strong under hers.

She watched now as Gray turned his truck around and drove back down South Willow heading toward Aspen. Since moving out of his father's house, he'd been staying in the Hotel Galena in Aspen.

But he'd be checking out soon enough, wouldn't he?

The following Saturday, Gray went to the Gingerbread House for what had become a weekly tradition, Adele's amazing gingerbread pancakes.

But this time would be different, now that he knew he was leaving. He hadn't seen or talked to Greta in the three days since the day of the closing, and he wasn't sure he should have come this morning. But Adele had called him the night before to make sure he was coming. He knew she loved making those pancakes for him, that it made her happy. And so he had come.

When Adele answered the door he was surprised to see an obviously forced smile fixed on her face. "Good morning," she said a little too breezily, but he knew her too well now to just go along with it.

"What's wrong, Adele? Where's Greta?"

"Upstairs, sleeping," Adele answered, as she closed the door behind him. Her gaze cut up to the ceiling where Greta's room was on the second floor, the phony smile falling away. "She's back where she used to be, Gray, back when she thought the house was lost. Sleeping a lot, not eating. Did something happen between you two?"

Gray's brows shot up. "She didn't tell you?"

"Tell me what?"

"I'm leaving."

"What?" He saw the surprise and hurt on her face, and it pained him to be causing it.

"I got a job offer in San Diego. And now that my dad's house is sold, I don't have any reason to stay."

"Yes, you do," Adele insisted, her gaze again finding the ceiling and Greta beyond it. "You two were made for each other."

Gray shook his head, sweeping a hand through his hair. "There's nothing I want more, but I can't be with her when she has such a wall up against me. I've tried for months to tear it down, and I just end up banging my head against it. It's like she's stuck there behind it, stagnant. Nothing I do or say changes anything. I just can't do it anymore. I love her too much."

Adele touched his arm. "But she *does* love you."

He lifted his shoulders in a resigned shrug. "I know that. Sometimes I can see it so clearly in her eyes. It's right there and I can almost touch it, but then that wall slides back down and it vanishes."

Adele's eyes grew rigid. "Damn that man for doing this to her." She let out a terse breath, her fingers twisting in her apron. "Sometimes I wish I could just . . . shake her. Shake some sense into her. Make her see what a good man you are."

Gray shook his head. "I'm sorry. I know you're frustrated too."

Adele's brown eyes suddenly took on a decidedly mischievous gleam. Gray cocked his head curiously. "What?"

Instead of answering, Adele cast her gaze over to the

Mainbocher dress hanging on a form in the bay window. Gray had suggested they put it on display as an example of their excellent beadwork. A little sign on the wall next to the door told his grandmother's story about Eleanor Broussard. Beside it was a "before" picture showing how it had looked after his little squirrel friends had their way with it.

Many a bride had asked if the dress were for sale in the last three months, but Gray refused any and all offers. He hadn't yet given up hope that he'd find a use for it. Maybe now it was time to consider selling, let some happy young bride shine in it.

"Why don't you come back to the kitchen?" Adele asked in a whisper. "I don't want Greta to hear this."

Gray was surprised to feel an amused grin flicker across his mouth. "Why, Adele Kelly, you look positively sneaky, you know that?"

Her eyes glinted with excitement. "I *feel* positively sneaky."

He followed her into the kitchen and sat down at the table. Adele sat across from him and leaned forward conspiratorially, her hands clasped together, her cheeks flushed wonderfully pink. "What are you doing next Saturday?"

Gray narrowed his eyes above a smile. "Why?"

"Oh, I've got a little idea."

"Okay, give," Gray said, grinning. He already knew he'd do whatever she wanted. Talk about nurturing happiness. She was absolutely beaming.

"I know my daughter, Gray. She can be the most stubborn thing on the planet. Sometimes she just needs a little persuasion, a little push in the right direction."

Gray raised his eyebrows. "What exactly do you have in mind?"

The mischievous look in Adele's eyes returned, intensified now, erasing a good twenty years from her face. "Maybe something good can come from this affliction of mine."

Chapter Thirty-three

I am really going to miss this dress," Adele said as she gazed at the Mainbocher one more time on the dress form before they packed it up for Gray.

Greta covered her mouth as she yawned. "It's not a pet, Mom."

"Oh, I know, but it's just so beautiful. It's like having art in your house for only a little while and then it's taken away."

"Well, he's leaving and he's taking it with him," Greta said and heard the flat pragmatism in the words. But that was all right. She didn't want to reveal the confused array of emotions that just saying the words had drummed up, not even to herself. Flat was just fine. Soon he'd be gone and that would be that. "Let's just get this over with."

Together, they worked the dress slowly up and off the form. Adele held the dress carefully as Greta brought over the acid-free storage box.

"Oh, Greta," her mother's singsong voice came at her as she opened the top of the box. *Uh-oh.* Her mother had used her I'm-about-to-ask-you-something-you're-probably-not-going-to-like voice.

Greta turned to see Adele smiling at her. "You know, one thing about art. It just hangs there." She nodded down at the dress. "I sure would like to see it in motion, just once."

Greta groaned. "Oh, Mom, no."

"Please? Just for a minute? I worked so hard on it. And it always looked so lifeless sitting there on the form."

Greta raised her palms. "It won't even fit me! It's way too small."

"Just try, okay? Please?"

Greta burst out a breath. "All right, Mom. But you owe me."

Shaking her head, Greta took the dress from her mother and headed upstairs to her bedroom to change.

"Oh, and put your hair up too, will you?" Adele called behind her. "And maybe some nice shoes? I want the full effect."

Greta only rolled her eyes.

The Mainbocher draped down over Greta's body in a luxurious wave of rich satin. She turned to look in the mirror. Gosh, what a dress. And it fit perfectly. She must have lost a little weight the past couple of weeks.

The next few minutes she spent tucking her curls into an impromptu updo. She wasn't used to fiddling much with her hair, and it took a bit longer than she'd thought. When she was done, she inspected herself in the mirror. Not bad. "Oh, what the heck," she muttered and put on some mascara and lipstick.

Now for shoes. She wasn't sure she had any that would be appropriate. Her selection was pretty meager. Good thing the dress was long enough to cover them up for the most part.

Her eyes widened when she saw a brand-new-looking pair of white pumps in the corner of her closet. When had she bought those? Shrugging, she pulled them out and slipped them on.

After one last glance in the mirror, she headed back to the stairs. Halfway down she paused. "Here we go, Mom. Ready?" Greta grinned, excited despite herself. Striding into the front room, she immediately struck a pose. "Ta-da!"

Her mother was gone. Greta whirled around to the door, saw it opened just a crack.

"Here we go again," she mumbled.

Tugging up the bottom of the dress, she headed outside and scanned the road in both directions. Adele was nowhere in sight. She couldn't have gotten too far.

Greta hurried back inside, grabbed her keys, and headed for the Bug. She climbed in carefully, mindful of the dress, and drove down South Willow, her eyes constantly scanning the road and side streets for her mother.

She hit the erstwhile candy shop first, but didn't spot Adele inside. She then headed toward a new place where she'd found her mother after one of her unscheduled excursions, the town's original school. The building had been converted to high-end condos in the late eighties. Two weeks before, Greta had found her mother sitting on the front steps baffled as to why the school doors were locked. She'd thought Greta was her second-grade teacher, Mrs. Conroy.

But Adele wasn't there today.

On to St. Luke's. Driving up to the church, Greta was surprised to see the parking lot filled with cars. It was Saturday today, right? Not Sunday. Was there some sort of an event there today? A baptism or a wedding? That would be odd. She usually heard if anything big was going on.

She managed to find a parking spot along the curb a half block down from the church, climbed out of the Bug, and hurried up the street, holding the hem of the dress off the ground.

She bustled up the front steps of the church and opened the enormous double doors, trying hard to be quiet, not wanting to interrupt. Her eyes widened when she found the church absolutely packed, everyone dressed to the nines. It was quiet inside except for a few soft murmurs and whispers.

Up front at the altar was Pastor Trane, beaming back toward her. In virtual unison, everyone else pivoted in their seats to look at her, so many familiar faces, each one of them smiling.

Greta blew out a breath in relief when she saw her mother step out from Pastor Trane's office. She'd changed and was now wearing a pale lavender dress suit that Greta had never seen before.

And there was Penny, following along behind Adele, in a champagne colored sheath dress with a bateau neckline. She'd lost much of the weight she'd gained from the birth of her baby two months earlier, an impressive feat considering that she worked in the best bakery in Pitkin County.

Greta's brow creased when she saw both Penny and her mother holding small but elegant bouquets tied with pale blue ribbons. The end of each pew was also adorned with a spray of white roses with ribbons the same pale shade of blue cascading down to the floor.

"Greta?" she heard softly from behind her and turned

to see Gray standing just outside the door, wearing a gorgeous three-piece tux, his dark hair smoothed back from his face and gleaming in the sun.

Every last bit of air in her lungs whooshed out, and Greta had to consciously remember to breathe as she stared at him, the black jacket of the tux intensifying the deep blue of his eyes into dark sapphires. His mouth was set in a thin straight line, not exactly smiling but not quite frowning.

"Wow, you look incredible," she whispered, and Gray's lips parted in a small smile.

"Hey, that's my line. But thanks." He took a step back and looked at her in the dress, his eyes so intent she felt her face warm in a self-conscious blush. "And you, Greta Kendall, are glorious in that dress." His gaze reached her face and he narrowed his eyes. "Are you wearing makeup?"

She nodded, feeling her cheeks flare up once again. Her brows creased, she gestured toward the inside of the church. "So, what's going on?"

Now Gray's mouth split in a wide-open smile, his eyes glittering. "What do you think? Our wedding."

Greta gasped, her eyes glued on his. "Our . . ."

"Wedding."

"Oh, but Gray—"

She stopped as he took a step closer to her, his smile falling away as he took her hand and spoke softly so that only she could hear him, all the while keeping his eyes riveted on hers.

"If you don't mind, I'd like to speak now not to the Greta that's standing here today, but to the Greta I know who's inside there, the one that was so very afraid that terrible day three months ago, the one who needed reassurance she'd never feel that way again." He squeezed her hand. "I want you to know that I will do everything in my power to protect you and make sure nothing ever hurts you. The thing is, though, I won't be alone in that. This Greta is here too."

Tears burned in Greta's eyes, but she said nothing.

"And even if she doesn't trust herself to protect you, *I* trust her to. I've gotten to know her pretty well this summer, and I can tell you she's stronger than she thinks. She's no longer a person capable of love so blind that she would allow someone to hurt her." He let out a light chuckle. "In fact, I'd feel sorry for anyone who tried. So even if she tells me to get lost today, I know I'm leaving you in good hands."

Greta covered her mouth with her hand as Gray dropped to one knee. From inside the church, she heard delighted giggles and murmurs. "But what I'd really like is for you to set her free, allow her to love again. See, I love her a lot and would like very much to marry her."

Greta shook her head. "Oh, Gray, I don't know—" But then she stopped. She did know, didn't she? Everything he'd said had been exactly right, exactly what she had needed to hear. And she hadn't even known he was aware of the "other Greta," the one she'd made the vow to in the bathroom that day as Mark waited just outside the door. But, of course, he knew.

She hadn't given him enough credit. Not nearly enough.

And so instead of protesting she found herself nodding. "Okay."

Gray burst out a rich, deep laugh. "Okay?"

She grinned. "Yes."

He rose and then turned to face the anxiously awaiting crowd in the church. "She said yes!"

Everyone cheered and hollered. Seeing them all so happy for her made tears once again brim and trickle down Greta's cheeks.

Chuckling softly, Gray wiped them away with his thumbs. "And we don't have to do this wedding thing right now. Your mom and I—well, we just wanted to give you a little—"

He stopped as she touched his arm. "No, I want to. I really do. I love you."

His eyes flashed dark, becoming the dangerous blue of an ocean under a stormy sky. "Say that again."

"I love you, Gray."

Leaning down to her, he brushed his lips against hers in a soft caress of a kiss.

"All right, then, let's do this. Come on, my dad's in there too. I want you to meet him."

Greta took his arm, but then she remembered. "What about San Diego?"

Gray lifted his shoulder in a half shrug. "I never gave them a definitive answer. Now I can."

She nodded and then tugged back on his arm. "And wait, don't we need a marriage license?"

Gray grinned. "Got it covered. Your friend LuAnne's in there."

Greta laughed. LuAnne Gibson was the town clerk and administrator of marriage licenses. She'd also been Greta's favorite babysitter as a little girl.

They entered the church, and everyone rose to their feet, watching as Greta and Gray walked down the aisle together, most blinking back happy tears.

Chapter Thirty-four

The ceremony was simple but heartfelt, and Gray heard plenty of sniffles from behind him. His eyes, too, had welled the moment he slipped the ring onto Greta's finger. She just looked so stunning standing there in his grandmother's Mainbocher, perfectly restored, the beads of the dress sparkling like an array of tiny diamonds.

Her wearing the gown really had made it feel as if his mother were here, if only in spirit. It was a shame she hadn't had the chance to meet Greta. They would have loved each other. His mother had never really taken to Stephanie, but had always tried to for Gray's sake.

After the ceremony, they returned to the Gingerbread House, where its immense backyard, really more of a meadow, served as a reception hall. Everyone brought a dish of something or other, enough to nearly overwhelm the two long tables Pastor Trane had brought over from the church.

Potluck in a small town. It just didn't get any better than that.

Gray and Greta had mingled with their guests for about an hour, and then they each filled a plate and made their way over to what Greta had told him was the best picnic spot in the meadow, a circle of soft grass tucked close to the edge of the aspen grove running along the stream. They'd laid out a plaid blanket and settled down to eat their very first meal together as husband and wife.

Overhead, the aspen leaves gleamed a brilliant gold under the early-autumn sun, the tops of the trees lit up in burnt orange and crimson red, as if they'd been dipped in flames. Luckily, the sun was still bright and warm enough during the day, although the nights were getting colder and colder. Still, it was a bit chilly in the shade of the trees, and Gray wrapped his tuxedo jacket around Greta's shoulders before sitting down next to her.

Now Gray shielded his eyes from the sun and scanned the throng of people by the house. He breathed out when he saw his father sitting on the steps of the back porch, with Adele seated beside him. Even from here, he could see the familiar blank expression on his dad's face. But at least he was here, maybe even aware of what was going on, although Gray knew that was probably only wishful thinking.

"They're fine," Greta said softly, touching his arm. "Penny's keeping an eye on them."

Gray nodded and turned his attention to his food, ready to dig in, his plate heaping with homemade macaroni and cheese, a healthy dollop of the Main Street Deli's apparently famous potato salad, and two plump brats fresh off the grill, proudly cooked by Todd Grindbold, "Master of the Grill," or so his apron proclaimed.

But this was just a sampling of the enormous quantity of food. Gray could have filled five plates and not doubled up on a single thing.

For a couple of minutes they ate in silence, but then

Gray sensed a growing tension coming from Greta. Curious, he watched her take a sip of the rich Spector Ale made by yet another old classmate of hers, Anton something, in what Gray had been told was officially the smallest brewery in Colorado. Greta eyed his plate, a small worried smile playing at the corners of her mouth.

"So," she began with a nervous laugh, "mac 'n' cheese and brats—not exactly the usual wedding fare, huh?"

Gray saw real worry edge into her eyes as she waited for his response. She thought he was disappointed, didn't she? She knew this was probably the polar opposite of what he and Stephanie had planned for their wedding.

That was actually true. Gray thought back to the endless taste testings, the parade of fancy hors d'oeuvres, the exquisitely prepared but miniscule-portioned entrées, the rivers of fine wine and expensive champagne. He winced, remembering the aftermath of those particular sessions.

But disappointed over this spread? No way.

Gray smiled, leaned in close to Greta, and touched the tip of her nose. "It's exactly perfect." She let out a relieved breath. "Besides," Gray continued with a shrug, "champagne gives me a headache."

From somewhere in the crowd came the *clink-clink-clink* of beer bottles tapping against each other, in lieu of silverware tapping against crystal flutes. Plastic forks didn't have quite the same effect.

Grinning, Gray glanced over at the guests. Every last one of them had turned to look and were now watching and smiling at them in an expectant hush.

"Kiss time," Gray murmured as he leaned in and kissed his beautiful bride, his lips lingering for an extra couple of seconds longer than could be called a *peck*. Everyone behind them whooped and cheered.

Greta laughed that wonderful natural laugh of hers. "Our lips are going to be swollen from all this kissing."

"Well, they'd better get used to it," Gray said, grinning. "There's going to be a whole lot of kissing in this marriage."

"Ooh, candid shot!" Ian Koslovsky suddenly jumped in front of them, camera at the ready, and clicked a picture of the startled couple. Distracted by the kiss, they hadn't seen him approaching.

Gregor came up right behind his brother, shaking his head. "You can't announce 'candid shot' like that and then take a picture. It makes it *not* candid anymore. Duh."

"They're my pictures," Ian grumbled. "I can do what I want."

"Fine, but I'm just saying, it's not candid anymore."

"Whatever." Ian glanced down at Greta. "I know you're going to like my pictures better, Greta."

"Nope," Gregor refuted with a quick shake of his head. "Mine."

Greta laughed. "I'm sure I'll like them both."

At that, they both let their cameras drop to their sides and frowned down at her.

"Well, that's no fun," Gregor said.

"Yeah. Sheesh, Greta," Ian said with equal disapproval. "You have to pick a winner."

Penny walked up behind both of them, with her baby, Charlotte, sleeping peacefully in her arms despite the racket of the party behind her. "All right, kids, it's cake time!"

The twins instantly brightened. "Photo op!" they said in unison.

Ian raised his eyebrows at his brother in a clear challenge. "Race you for the best spot?"

Gregor smiled. "You're on!"

"Ready, set, go!" they shouted together, and suddenly they were off, tearing through the meadow back toward the house where the cake table was being set up by the grill.

"Is everything a competition with those two?" Gray asked as he helped Greta up.

"Yup," Penny said, smiling as she watched the two grown men in somewhat rumpled suits running full-throttle through the meadow like little boys.

"They've always been like that," Greta said.

Penny touched Greta's arm. "Oh, did you hear? They're combining the papers again."

"Oh, great," Greta said. "I knew that wouldn't last."

Gray looked down at Charlotte, her thick lashes fluttering against her chubby cheeks. Without even thinking about it, he leaned over and just barely grazed the side of her little face with his thumb.

He caught Penny's wink at Greta. "I hope I'll be congratulating the two of you on a certain little something pretty quick here."

Greta's face flushed a charming rosy pink. "Maybe," she murmured, then cast a quick shy glance at Gray that sent a fresh rush of pure love surging through his heart.

"Wait 'til you see the cake," Penny gushed as they headed back to the house. "I did the roses myself."

Greta flashed another smile at Gray. "Roses are her specialty."

"Ah," Gray said, nodding.

He'd become very fond of Greta's friend while planning the wedding together these last few days, along with Adele.

As they approached the back porch, Penny's dad and two brothers emerged from the back door carrying the cake.

Everyone in the crowd gasped, and Gray's mouth dropped open. It was the most beautiful cake he'd ever seen. And he'd seen a lot of them. Of all the wedding choices, Stephanie had been the pickiest about the cake. Of course she'd selected the most expensive one they'd seen. Gray had thought the actual cake a bit bland and on the dry side, but apparently that hadn't mattered. It looked good.

But *this* cake surpassed even that one, a five-tiered monster, brilliant white frosting covered with light blue and silver icing swirled together in an impossibly intricate pattern. A spray of white roses spiraled down around the tiers, completely encircling the bottom tier. It was absolutely breathtaking.

Gray's eyes shifted to Greta beside him, and his heart fluttered in his chest. As beautiful as the cake was, it paled in comparison to the way Greta looked in this moment, her gaze riveted on the magnificent cake, her face radiating happiness, cheeks flushed, lips parted in a wide-open smile. But it was her eyes that made his heart sing, the brown of them shining gloriously, glints of gold in them sparkling in the sunlight.

His *wife*.

She seemed to sense him staring at her. She looked up at him, and he saw tears brimming in her eyes. A trickle escaped down her cheek and Gray smiled, reaching over to wipe it gently away with his thumb. He leaned in close to her.

"I love you," he murmured in her ear, soft and low, meant only for her to hear.

More tears escaped as Greta burst out a laugh of sheer delight.

Chapter Thirty-five

Hearing him say the words still surprised her, delicious tingles tickling her belly each and every time.

"I love you too," she whispered back.

Greta felt a little shy saying the words, still feeling as if she shouldn't say them, that they were still forbidden. But she would get over that.

She turned to Penny, who was anxiously awaiting a response to the astonishing cake her family had created. "Oh, Pen, it's so beautiful. It's just perfect."

Penny beamed. "Really?"

"Really. All of it." Greta knew Penny, Gray, and her mother had put this little shindig together, all of them co-conspirators. "So much work, though, and you've got your hands full with Charlotte."

Penny shrugged. "To see you this happy? Are you kidding me? But enough of this gushy stuff. There's a cake here in need of cutting."

"Yes, ma'am," Greta said with a quick salute.

Together, she and Gray cut out the first piece and laid it out on a small paper plate. Greta smiled, seeing it was her favorite, buttermilk spice cake. As Penny well knew.

Greta scooped up a forkful and fed it to Gray. His eyes widened. "Wow." He shook his head in amazement. "Now not only have I had the best pancakes on the planet in the fine town of Spector, Colorado, but now the best cake too."

"And beer!" Anton shouted out from the crowd.

Gray laughed. "Okay, the best beer too."

As Penny and her brothers cut up the cake and passed it around, Gray and Greta enjoyed their shared piece.

For a moment Gray just looked out at the sea of faces in front of them, every last one of them smiling. "Is it possible to be jealous of a whole town?"

Greta frowned, not understanding.

"Everyone here loves you. Do you realize that?"

Greta shrugged. "I think Spector loves a good party. That's why they're here."

"No," Gray said, and he wasn't smiling anymore. "They're here for you. They love you."

Greta turned around and looked at the crowd gathered around them, so many people. And scanning their faces, she realized she knew every single one of them.

And Gray was right. They did love her, didn't they? And she loved them.

Fresh tears sprang to her eyes as it finally hit her. That's what made Spector Spector, wasn't it? The people and the love they all shared for one another. And that was something a new mall wouldn't—*couldn't* change.

And then Greta found herself grinning to herself through her tears. She had to admit she did love a warm, gooey Cinnabon every now and again.

"What?" Gray asked, curious, seeing her goofy smile.

"Nothing," Greta said, wiping tears off her cheeks for the hundredth time. "I'm just happy, that's all."

And then came the *clink-clink-clink* of beer bottles again, dozens of them.

"Oh, no, not again," Gray said with exaggerated dread.

Greta grinned and leaned close to him. "Suffer," she whispered, and this time she kissed *him*.

Epilogue

Gray flipped the last pancake expertly onto the warming plate and dabbed some butter on it so it would melt into the fluffy center. He knocked on the window, and Greta looked up from her vegetable patch. "Breakfast's ready," he mouthed.

She nodded, smiling, and stood up, wiping her hands on her overalls.

Gray turned and headed down the hall to Adele's workroom. There sat Adele and six-year-old Julia, as usual huddled together over the wooden worktable.

Greta and Gray had named their daughter after Gray's mother. His father had cried when they'd told him during one of his rare lucid moments. He'd passed away the year before, and Gray still missed him very much.

It was nice having Adele here, despite having to watch as the Alzheimer's took an increasingly firm hold on her mind. She still had many lucid times, though. During one of them, she'd taught him how to make the gingerbread pancakes he loved so much.

After many failed attempts, he'd finally mastered them and had taken to calling himself "Master of the Griddle."

For a moment, he just looked at the two of them, both

humming contentedly, the same little tune he'd always heard from Adele.

Julia was the spitting image of Greta, except her tumble of curls was a shade darker than Greta's and she had Gray's blue eyes. Also unlike Greta, Julia had picked up on the art of beading almost immediately when Adele began teaching her, her small fingers now expertly grasping the tiny spheres and maneuvering them onto the strands with an assurance and confidence that belied her age. Her favorite place in the world now was right here in her grandmother's workroom. The two of them spent many happy hours in there together.

Adele looked up now and smiled at him. "Oh, hello there. I'm Adele."

Gray smiled, although it was always a little bittersweet when she didn't recognize him. "Hi, Adele. I'm Gray."

Adele glanced fondly over at Julia. "This is my daughter, Greta. Isn't she beautiful?"

Just then Greta came down the hall, pulling off her work gloves, her curls messy in a wind-blown ponytail, a smudge of dirt on her cheek and chin.

"Oh, yes, she is," he said, gazing at this woman he loved so very much. "She most certainly is."